Alan Hunter was born in Hoveton, Norfolk, in 1922. He left school at the age of fourteen to work on his father's farm, spending his spare time sailing on the Norfolk Broads and writing nature notes for the *Eastern Evening News*. He also wrote poetry, some of which was published while he was in the RAF during the Second World War. By 1950, he was running his own book shop in Norwich and in 1955, the first of what would become a series of forty-six George Gently novels was published. He died in 2005, aged eighty-two.

The Inspector George Gently series

Gently Does It
Gently by the Shore
Gently Down the Stream
Landed Gently
Gently Through the Mill
Gently in the Sun
Gently with the Painters
Gently to the Summit
Gently Go Man

Gently with the Painters

Alan Hunter

ROBINSON

Constable & Robinson Ltd
55–56 Russell Square
London WC1B 4HP
www.constablerobinson.com

This paperback edition published by Robinson,
an imprint of Constable & Robinson Ltd, 2011

A copy of the British Library Cataloguing in
Publication Data is available from the British Library

ISBN: 978-1-78033-144-7

Typeset by TW Typesetting, Plymouth, Devon

Printed and bound in the UK

3 5 7 9 10 8 6 4 2

To
THE NORWICH TWENTY GROUP
OF PAINTERS
Who suggested, but are not portrayed as,
the Palette Group of the novel.

CHAPTER ONE

HUSBAND AT POLICE STATION
FOR THREE HOURS
Victim's Picture in Exhibition
Yard to be called?

F OR THREE MORNINGS now Gently had been turning to this news item with an eagerness which, in spite of himself, had continued to grow steadily. And now, for the first time, the ominous words had been invoked: at last they had mentioned Scotland Yard.

He folded back the paper and propped it against his teapot. Of the two photographs reproduced one was a print which had been heavily retouched. This depicted the husband being escorted into the police station; he was a burly, heavy-featured man, with fair wavy hair and a Bomber Command moustache. The other showed a watercolour with a number on its frame – a pale, somewhat indefinite picture of a figure striding through driving rain.

'Mr Johnson Arriving At The Police Station Yesterday.'

'The Last Picture Painted By Shirley Johnson.'

1

At the foot of the column a smaller photograph was cut in. It was of St John Mallows, RA, with whose features Gently was familiar. He was the chairman of the Palette Group of which Shirley Johnson had been a member, and he had gone to press with the statement that her picture would certainly remain on show. Why not, when it was guaranteed to treble the attendance . . . ?

About Gently the established routine of his morning continued its methodical course. After twenty years in his Finchley rooms he went through the ritual with little conscious direction. When he had bathed and shaved he took a walk down the garden – it wasn't very far, up there in Finchley! – and then he would stand for a moment in Mrs Jarvis's kitchen, exchanging a few words of domestic commonplace.

'There's a bit of fly on those roses of yours . . .'

'I know, Mr Gently, Fred was only saying last night . . .'

'Have you been to the Golder's Green Hip this week?'

'Oh yes, Mr Gently. Me and Olive went on Tuesday.'

Then he went to his room, where the table was set. His mail and his papers always lay beside his plate. There were the usual bills and perhaps a letter from his sister; he would conscientiously read it first before turning to the news.

For six days in the week it went on like that, whenever he wasn't called out on a case. It formed a sort of hors d'oeuvre, an appetizer to the day, and he was always irritable if something interrupted it. And now, very delicately, something had. That business about the Johnsons had taken a hold on his imagination. It had occurred in the district on which he was regarded as a specialist, and more and more he had the feeling that the case belonged to him.

It belonged to him – but he wasn't going to get it! At least, that was the impression he'd received since Tuesday. There was nothing in the press reports to suggest that the local police were flagging, and really, it looked an open and shut case against the husband. He didn't have an alibi that held any water. He was admittedly estranged from his arty wife. They lived together in a flat about a mile from the scene of the crime, but they lived in separation, sleeping and eating in separate rooms . . .

'What would you like to follow, Superintendent?'

That was something else which took a little swallowing. Though he had known it was coming for several months in advance, his promotion had nevertheless caught him off-balance. In a number of subtle ways it was affecting his personality. He no longer felt entirely at home with himself. Shamefacedly, he had bought some new suits and an expensive trilby, while he was thinking of parting with the old Riley in the garage. How was it that an external like rank had this effect on him?

'Some of the liver you were frying . . . were there any letters for me?'

'Go on, Mr Gently! You've put your grapefruit on them.'

And also, he remembered, he had cut his outing in the garden. With his mind fixed on the Johnsons he'd gone straight down to the breakfast table, barely pausing at the door to wish Mrs Jarvis a good morning. Was it intuition, perhaps? He read the relevant passage again. The local police had not committed themselves, but the reporter had smelt a rat. That case, apparently so watertight, had somewhere sprung a leak.

As he ate his liver and bacon he let his eye stray down the column. After the hottest news, as usual, there came a résumé of the affair.

'The questioning of Johnson follows the grim discovery on Tuesday. The body of his wife, pretty Shirley Johnson, was found behind dustbins on the City Hall car park. She was stabbed with a steel letter opener which was found still plunged in the body. The discovery was made by an old-age pensioner as he returned from the early morning fruit and vegetable auction held at the cattle market. He informed the City Police who have placed Chief Inspector Hansom, CID, in charge of the investigation.

'It is established that the victim was attacked shortly after leaving a meeting of the Palette Group on the Monday evening. The Palette Group is composed of a number of local artists under the chairmanship of the well-known landscape painter, Charles St John Mallows, RA. The members meet on the first Monday of each month in the cellar of the George III public house, only a short distance from the scene of the crime. At the meetings they exhibit their work for criticism. They hold an annual exhibition in the nearby Castle Gardens.

'Charles St John Mallows, RA, interviewed by our reporter, described Mrs Johnson as being one of the most talented members of the Group. Asked about the meeting on Monday, he declined to make any statement other than that it contained 'the average amount of cut and thrust'. According to an independent source, the Palette Group meetings are noted for their frankness and forthright opinions.

'Derek Paul Johnson, the husband, is an estate agent in the city. During the war he served in the RAF and was

4

shot down over Cologne while piloting a Lancaster bomber. He was a prisoner of war in Germany for two years.'

It wasn't difficult to see where the reporter's fancy was leading him. He was selling the notion of a blood feud at the Palette Group. Johnson's grilling was news and had to make up the headline, but the pedal of sympathy had been touched in the last paragraph. Was it the Palette Group that was worrying Inspector Hansom, too?

For a moment Gently was tempted to put a call through to Hansom, then he shrugged and hurried up with his marmalade and toast. It wasn't his business yet, and perhaps it wasn't going to be. Since they'd made him a Super he was being kept more at home; he had seen several likely jobs being handed on to his juniors.

'I've ordered a joint for tonight, Superintendent. Do you know if you'll be home for dinner?'

He shouldn't have been irritated by that reasonable question, and yet he wanted to snap at Mrs Jarvis. All the way on the Tube he was brooding over the Johnsons. They clogged him up the Embankment from Charing Cross Station.

It was the beginning of July, and fine weather to boot, with the surface of the Thames a-dazzle in a bright sun. Several of Gently's colleagues were away on vacation, and his own was due in a fortnight's time. For the first week he was going to Bridgit in Wiltshire – a family sacrifice this, since his brother-in-law bored him. But the second week he was spending at a fishing inn in the Fens, near where, according to report, there were big bream and plenty.

A whole week of fishing! He'd been dreaming about it since Easter, when, while out on a case, he'd first heard about the spot. He had made a few inquiries and booked a room at the Fenman's Arms. A local angler who had figured in the case was going to join him for the weekend.

He thought about it now as he walked by the morning Thames, but somehow a little of the glamour seemed to have departed from the prospect. He knew he was being childish to want the Johnson case made over to him: he couldn't help it, the habit was stuck there – once, he would have got it automatically.

On the stairs he was passed by Pagram, who carried a box-file under his arm.

'The AC's looking for you – he wants the dope on Jimmy Fisher.'

'Anything come in from the country?'

'If it has I haven't heard about it. Hoskins was briefed for that job at Plymouth, but I dare say you heard that yesterday.'

'It shouldn't be too difficult.'

'Hoskins has got a flair for hold-ups.'

Gently went grumpily on his way. Hoskins was a young-and-coming Inspector. He had made a name for himself in a case where a sub-postmistress had been coshed to death, since when he was number one for any business of that description. And there were several young-and-coming Inspectors in Homicide, all eager to grab any plums that were going . . .

He banged into his office and pulled down the file on Fisher. This was the sort of job which they were finding for him these days! A long, complicated affair that revolved round the warehouse rackets, becoming Homicide's pigeon only when a hot suspect was shot. It had been going on now for a couple of months, raids, tip-offs and a few unimportant arrests. Pagram and he were both working on it, and, it seemed, half the Metropolitan Police besides. Routine wasn't his strong point, and the AC ought to know it . . . How did they expect him to get his teeth into a diffuse business of this kind?

'Ah, Gently. Is that the Fisher file?'

The Assistant Commissioner was looking pleased with himself. He was a spare, genial man with horn-rimmed spectacles, and had always reminded Gently of an amiable schoolmaster.

'You know, I think we're going to crack that case at last. Limehouse had a tip-off last night, and it's really put our hands on something. You remember Herbie the Fence? The little man with all the answers? Well, just look out that report, will you, and the interrogations of Wilbright and Sharp . . .'

In effect it had been a tip-off that Herbie had got the goods on him, and Limehouse Division had raided his premises. In a cellar they had discovered some of the furs which had been stolen, furs originating from the warehouse where Jimmy Fisher had been shot. Herbie was sitting in the cooler waiting for Gently's expert attention: he hadn't been charged with anything and so was free meat for the chopper.

'Take your time over him, Gently, take all the time in the world. If we can crack Herbie we'll have the whole consignment sewn up . . .'

So there it was, his day mapped out for him, another day

with Jimmy Fisher. Not a word about jobs in the country, not a whisper of Inspector Hansom . . .

Gently returned to his office dourly and made arrangements for the interrogation. Herbie and he had had previous engagements, and even equipped with a lever, he knew what he was in for. At lunchtime he handed the business over to Pagram, with Herbie, still uncracked, going as strongly as ever. From the canteen he sent out for the lunchtime papers. They contained mostly rehashes, but there was one fresh development.

PUBLIC SEE THE JOHNSON PICTURE
Angry Scene At Exhibition

With his fork in his hand, Gently skimmed the column of letterpress. Only one paper had got it, and judging from the misprints it had been a rush job:

Ruction and tumult disturbed this old Cathedral City when the Palette Group's Summer Exhibition was opened this morning. Cause of the contention was Shirley Johnson's 'Dark Destroyer', the last picture she was known to have painted before she was murdered.

The exhibition was opened by the Lord Mayor, Mr Ted Brownlow. He recalled that the district had produced the only provincial school of painting.

Almost before he had finished speaking a noisy argument broke out, apparently between one or two members of the Group.

Others joined in and the argument became a row. Fists were waved and there was threatening behaviour.

Police intervened to prevent a probable fight, and the most heated of the participants were escorted from the exhibition.

One of them told our reporter that the trouble arose from the Johnson exhibit. He refused to explain how it had caused the dispute.

A public apology for the members' behaviour was made by Chairman St John Mallows, RA, who observed that it was not unknown for artists to hold strong opinions.

Not very hopefully Gently turned to the stop-press, but his luck was in and there was an intriguing postscript:

JOHNSON PICTURE – LATEST. Police have taken possession of picture [See Page One for full report].

He read it through again to make sure that he had missed nothing, but this was all that the paper could tell him. Again he was on the point of putting through a call to Hansom, but shamed himself from doing it when it came to the push. Hansom, he knew, wouldn't be too pleased to hear from him; he had twice in the past stolen the local man's thunder.

Back in the office Pagram took him to one side:

'I think our friend Herbie is contemplating a deal. He's harping now on how dangerous it would be for him to talk – he loves the police like brothers, of course, but he's got to think of his widowed mother. His get-out is still that another man rents his cellar.'

'I wish they'd given him a bath before they brought him up here.'

It was two hours later when Herbie laid out his cards. The procedure was delicate, though understood by both sides. In return for certain facts Herbie wanted his story accepted, but Gently wanted the facts before he agreed to consider the story. At last Herbie consented to give an outline of those facts, and Gently, with Pagram, had a huddle with the Assistant Commissioner. It then remained to get Herbie's statement and to set the wheels in motion. Within twenty-four hours, perhaps, they would know if the *coup* had been successful.

In his office, now cleared of Herbies, Gently drank coffee and filled his pipe. He would have given a lot to have known what they had finally done with Jimmy Fisher. He had been put on the case almost as soon as he had been promoted: the whole of his superintending seemed to have been linked with that epic inquiry. And was this how it was going to go on now that he had reached administrative rank? Until the day of his retirement, was he to be crucified on routine?

Puffing rings across his varnished desk, he began to realize what had happened to him. It was no longer the simple augmentation of rank which he had always seemed able to take in his stride. It was different, this; it was the crossing of a Rubicon. It had slammed a door on nearly three decades of his career. Before, in some sort, he had been a rebel, at least a stubborn and unmovable individualist. He had kicked against the Establishment that hampered and disagreed with him; he had seen himself as standing a little apart from it.

And that had continued from stage to stage, with never any need for a revision of attitude. From Detective

Constable to Chief Inspector he had remained the rebel within the gates. But now – almost treacherously – the case had altered; the rebel had been embodied as part of the Establishment. Without him for the moment having perceived what was done, he'd been jockeyed up to the line, his rebel teeth had been extracted. Unbelievably, he was one of them: he was on the other side of the fence.

Unbelievably! He stirred his feet in an access of irritation. As yet he couldn't accept this sleight-of-hand which had been worked on him. He was in a state of flux, neither one thing nor the other, and just at the moment he couldn't believe that he would ever settle again.

'Desk Sergeant here, sir.'

Gently grabbed the phone up sulkily.

'There's a man here, name of Tulkings, wants to see you on urgent business.'

'Is it about his long-lost nephew?'

'Don't know, sir. He wouldn't tell me.'

'If it is, say I've gone to America.'

'Yes, sir. I'll get rid of him.'

Another time it would be Mad Jenkins, or the widow from Bethnal Green. There was a floating congregation of crackpots who spent their time in harrying Scotland Yard.

'Super? This is Morris at this end.'

Gently sighed and prepared to be intelligent. Morris was an Inspector on a job in Walsall; just as Gently used to do, he was ringing in for information.

'. . . So I'd like anything you can get on this chap Polson. I'm pretty certain he's the chummie who knocked off Steen. If you could send a man to make inquiries at Shoreditch . . .'

'Get those prints off, will you?'

'They'll be in tonight, Super.'

In his desk Gently had a portable and he flicked it on to get the news, but the BBC, true to form, took notice of nothing so paltry as homicide. Another day had elapsed . . . had Hansom risked it and arrested Derek Johnson?

Immediately the phone was ringing again:

'Old man?'

It was Pagram, from the AC's office.

'We've got a tip-off about another warehouse raid, said to be by the same lot who perforated Jimmy. Limehouse again – could you come along up?'

Gently groaned and tapped out his pipe.

This time the conference was shorter and more decided. Limehouse and the Flying Squad were going to handle the job between them. The details were worked out over a large-scale plan, and on his wall-map the AC added one of the coloured flags he was so fond of.

'You see how they stick to those same three districts? It all gives support to what Herbie was telling us . . .'

Stephens, of Homicide, had sat in on the conference, but his failure to contribute to it suggested that he was there for something else. He chewed at his nails and occasionally stared at Gently. As the conference was breaking up he came forward with an expectant air.

'Oh, Stephens . . . Gently, hold on a tick!'

The AC rested his hand on Gently's arm.

'There's a job come up in your old hunting grounds. I'm putting Stephens on it, and I thought you could give him some tips.'

As far as Gently was concerned that was the very last

straw, and it was no use reminding himself that he had expected it. For an instant, looking at Stephens, he felt all of his fifty-two years: he felt himself pensioned off, to make room for these brisk newcomers.

'The Johnson case . . . ?'

'You've been reading about it, have you?'

'I did chance to see something . . .'

'Then you've got an idea of the set-up. From what I can make out the local police are in a tizzie. They've already stampeded themselves into doing something silly. You know about the picture? The damn fools have gone and impounded it, and from what I can hear they haven't a notion as to why they've done it. Now, of course, they want us to carry it, in the old, familiar fashion. I immediately thought of Stephens, who has got a cool enough head on his shoulders.'

Gently leant himself against the desk, feeling the need of its support. Of course, it had to be Stephens – wasn't it as plain as anything could be? Gently was Jimmy Fisher's man, the racketeer's *manes* were still unplacated. While he was stuck with Lucky Jim there couldn't be any trips into the country . . .

'Three months ago I'd have sent you, Gently.'

Had the AC divined his disappointment?

'As it is I dare say they'll expect you to go, which will probably make it tougher for Stephens here. But they'll have to learn to get on without our celebrities – obviously, you weren't going to remain a CI for ever. So, if you'll just give Stephens a little off-the-record briefing, we'll leave you in peace with the unlamented James Fisher.'

'I wouldn't have minded . . .'

The words stuck in his throat, but somehow he felt that he had to get them out.

'The way things are going . . . Pagram can probably manage. Though I don't want to stand in anyone's way . . .'

The AC looked at him in mild surprise, his spectacles dangling from his hand. Hadn't it really occurred to him that Gently might want the case, that he was loathing every moment of his office-bound routine?

'Well, in that case, Gently, what can I say?'

He shot a glance at Stephens, who was standing by impassively.

'I quite agree that the Fisher business is falling into place, and if you're agreeable, you're the very man for the other. Am I to understand that you'd like to have the case?'

As though he needed to ask it! Gently nodded dumbly.

'In that case it's yours – oh, and you'd better take Stephens with you. I know that Dutt is your regular man, but I think that Stephens will be of more use to you.'

It was a judgement of Solomon, and Gently was in no mood to question it. Neither, it seemed, was Stephens, who swallowed but said not a word. The AC handed them a folder containing a copy of the report, then dismissed them with a perfunctory 'Good night' which still contained a note of surprise in it.

Closeted with Gently in his office, Stephens became apologetic. He had an uncomfortable feeling that he had made a gaffe and created a bad impression with Gently.

'I can't say how glad I am that you've taken it. I was dreading having to go there, treading in your footsteps . . .'

'Don't worry about that.'

'It's a relief, I can tell you. I expect you know that I've only had two cases out of town . . .'

In the end, Gently found himself quite liking this young man. He had a proper sense of his own inadequacies and an even properer respect for his elders and betters. An engaging young man – one who would probably go far! Gently began to feel an almost avuncular regard for him.

'At Liverpool Street, then?'

It was past eight o'clock. In his satisfaction, Gently had not forgotten to phone Mrs Jarvis.

'No – come to my place. We'll drive down for a change.'

'It's Finchley, isn't it – Elphinstow Road?'

It wouldn't have surprised Gently even if Stephens had known the number.

CHAPTER TWO

AFTER HIS OFFICE-bound routine of the last few months Gently was possessed of a guilty feeling, as though he were off on a secret spree. As he was shaving he made ridiculous faces in the mirror, and several times he caught himself grinning idiotically at nothing. A shadow had been lifted, the shadow of new responsibilities. Once more he was off on his own cherished authority. Like a virtuoso, who, for a time, has been obliged to assist the orchestra, he was released again to his independent rhapsodies.

'And some they whistled, and some they sang.'

The most nonsensical of things kept running through his mind. At breakfast he astounded Mrs Jarvis by reciting a verse from a ballad, though why it should seem so apposite he couldn't have explained, even to himself.

'Are you going to be away for long, Superintendent?'

She regarded him, he noticed, with a blend of reproval and concern. Stephens, who arrived early, had brought an enormous suitcase with him. His face shone as though he had scrubbed it and he had recently clipped his small, downy moustache.

'I've been thinking the case over . . .'

Gently gave him a cup of tea. In the morning papers, he had been glad to see, there had been no recurrence of the 'calling the Yard' theme. Their space had been largely given to the exhibition and to the mysterious picture. Handsome Hansom had had his photograph taken along with the Lord Mayor and Charles St John Mallows.

By half past eight the Riley was outside and their luggage deposited in the boot. Mrs Jarvis had made a packet of sandwiches from last night's neglected joint, and this, with a couple of thermoses, she gave into the care of Stephens.

'Just see that the Superintendent eats something . . .'

She stood at her gate to watch them departing. It was a brilliant morning with a few scanty clouds, and the early traffic had not yet become troublesome.

'I thought you'd expect me to do a little work on it, sir. I've made a few notes of points which occurred to me. Of course, it's too early to be certain of anything . . .'

Nevertheless, Stephens had already propounded a theory to himself.

'If we rule out the husband – and the local police seem to have done it – then I'd say, sir, that we ought to look out for signs of blackmail. There's this St John Mallows – she might have had her hooks into him, and he must have been near the spot at the time she was murdered.'

'What do you think she had on him?' The youngster's zeal amused Gently.

'Well, sir, they might have been intimate together.'

'But St John Mallows isn't married.'

'No, but she is, sir. Then there might have been perversity, or something of that kind.'

17

Had it all seemed so easy when Gently was a young Inspector? Looking back, he couldn't remember ever having been very sure of himself. But that, possibly, was just the difficulty which Stephens was trying to counter; he was rushing at the case and searching feverishly for a pattern in it.

'That's something which we shall have to bear in mind, of course.'

'Yes, sir. I could almost swear – if we can once rule out the husband!'

'At the same time . . . by the way, here's Tally-ho Corner. I suppose you never read up the Rouse case, did you?'

It was as he had thought – Stephens was desperately unsure of himself. He welcomed the opportunity to switch the conversation elsewhere. The Rouse case, fortunately, was one that he had swotted up, and he talked about it readily as they made their way through Barnet and Hatfield.

'If he'd kept out of the witness-box, sir – that was his undoing. They'd never have hanged him on the evidence alone.'

'I imagine that the prosecution were banking on that. Knowing Rouse, they were pretty certain that he would take the stand.'

'Do you think so, sir? Was it a legitimate gamble?'

At Newmarket, where they stopped for coffee, Stephens insisted on receiving and paying the bill. He was smoking a pipe which, Gently noticed, was a sandblast much like his own in pattern. It was nearly new, with an unscratched mouthpiece. He couldn't remember whether he had seen Stephens smoking a pipe before or not.

'Like to try some of mine?'

He pushed across his tin of navy-cut. Stephens accepted a couple of slices and maladroitly stuffed his pipe with them. From the awkward manner he had of holding his pipe while he was smoking, Gently deducted that this was the young detective's first essay in the art . . .

By noon they were in the outskirts of the old provincial capital, familiar to Gently if not to his protégé. It possessed a fine approach along a wide and tree-lined carriageway, on either side of which stood attractive houses in well-kept grounds.

'Aren't the Northshire people rather difficult to get on with? Someone was telling me in the canteen . . .'

Gently smiled at the keep of the Norman castle, now lifting distantly above the rooftops.

'Don't pay attention to all you hear! You'll find them much the same as the rest.'

'But you're the expert on these parts—'

'You'll be one too, before we've finished the case.'

And Stephens, biting on his pipe, tried to look as though he believed he would.

At Police HQ, Superintendent Walker was waiting for them. Gently introduced Stephens to him and there followed the usual bout of shaking hands. A constable was dispatched to summon Chief Inspector Hansom, who, two minutes later, appeared still eating a ham sandwich.

'I thought they'd have sent someone else, now that you'd reached the giddy heights!'

Gently shrugged, finding a seat for himself beside Walker's desk. Between himself and Hansom there had ever been an armed neutrality; they were antipathetic towards each other, and yet, oddly enough, exerted a mutual fascination.

'You've had Hansom's report, Gently . . . where would you like him to begin?'

It was very nearly lunchtime, and the Super was eager to get to their business. Hansom, eating largely to get rid of the sandwich, had dumped himself clumsily at the other end of the desk. There wasn't a chair for Stephens and so he was obliged to remain standing; he stationed himself behind Gently, where he kept uncomfortably shifting his feet.

'I'd better begin at the beginning, which was about six a.m. on Tuesday. Sergeant Walters, who was on the desk, saw this old fool, Coles, hanging around. He'd been out there for half an hour, just loitering about and doing nothing; every time Walters went to the window he turned his back, or fiddled with a shoelace . . .'

Gently knew the type referred to and had given them a private cognomen: they were the 'angry old men', of whom every town could show some examples. Seedy, shabby and without any friends, they haunted the market places and busiest streets; they wore an expression of angry surprise, as though perpetually indignant at their age and poverty. And always, if anyone caught their eye, they furiously frowned and turned away . . .

'Walters went out and accosted the old idiot, wanting to know why he was hanging about there. He says it took him a good ten minutes to get anything intelligible out of the fellow. In the end he said, he supposed that Walters knew all about her – Walters said "Who?" – and this article said: "The sick lady"!

'He'd found Shirley Johnson with a knife sticking out of her shoulderblades, and that was the nearest he could get to describing her!'

So Walters had followed the old man into the car park, which, ironically enough, adjoined Headquarters as well as the City Hall; and there, behind the dustbins in which the ancient had come to forage, he found that very sick lady lying stiff in the morning dew.

'When you're ready, if you like, I'll take you round and show you the spot, but you'll see how we found her in these photographs here. There wasn't a lot of blood owing to the knife being left in, but we found one or two splashes leading from a spot about ten yards away.

'He simply stabbed her, I imagine, and then lugged her over to the dustbins. As you see here, he chucked her handbag and coat down beside her. She wasn't tampered with or mussed up and there were twenty pounds in her bag – likewise her driving licence, so we had no trouble in tracing her.'

Gently nodded, accepting the proffered bunch of glossy prints. They were interestingly gruesome, but not notably informative. The bins were standing by a terrace wall which flanked the large and much-used park, and though by day they offered little concealment, they would be effective enough after dark. The body had been carelessly dumped behind them. It had fallen on its face and had the right arm twisted beneath it. The thin handle of the paper knife protruded from below the left shoulderblade, and on it, in close up, one could read the inscription: 'Pearson Cutlers, Sheffield, Eng.' Only a small stain had appeared on the light-coloured dress.

'Did you find any prints?'

Gently handed the pictures to Stephens. The young man examined them with a painstaking thoroughness.

'Only hers, on the handbag. Chummie must have been wearing gloves. The handle hadn't been wiped, it just didn't have anything on it. There were some contusions on the throat which the Doc says were made before death, so it looks as though he were taking care that she didn't scream when she got the knife. Anyway, nobody heard her scream, and there would have been enough people about. According to the Doc she was killed between ten p.m. and midnight.'

'What time did she leave this artists' meeting?'

'Some time after ten-thirty, say twenty to eleven. She stayed talking outside with Mallows and maybe some of the others, then went off alone in the direction of her bus stop.'

'That's the one beside the car park?'

'Yes, the City Hall stop. It can't be more than a couple of hundred yards from the George III. You go up a flight of steps and then along the front of the City Hall, then turn left into St Saviour's, and there's the stop, nearly under the clock-tower. The bus she went after was an eighty-eight, which leaves that stop at ten to eleven.'

'But she didn't catch it, of course.'

'Yeah – so we narrow things down to ten minutes.'

'Were there no witnesses in the car park?'

'Two we've got, and they didn't see a sausage.'

The Super put in: 'It just missed the theatre turn-out. It's the patrons of the Playhouse who mostly use that park of an evening. Only half an hour earlier and the place

22

would have been crowded, but they've all got away by twenty to eleven.'

'What about people using the bus stop?'

Hansom extended a pair of none-too-clean hands.

'How do you make them come forward, that's what I'd like to know! We've appealed in the press a couple of times, but all it brought us was an old tabby with a complaint about a conductor. By her account there were six or seven other people waiting, but that's the beginning and end of her information.'

Gently nodded and drew some patterns on the desk with his finger. This murderer had either been lucky, or else very clever. He had committed his crime in the most improbable of places, and yet, by chance or plan, seemed to have got completely away with it.

'The buildings bordering the park – was nothing seen or heard from them?'

'Police HQ, I suppose you mean . . . ! Well, we didn't, so there you are. From the back here, I daresay, we could have watched from a score of windows – we could have done, but we didn't. We don't expect chummies down there!'

'You've got to remember that it was dark,' added the Super. 'The car park isn't lit and the nearest lights are in St Saviour's. To see anything going on you'd need to put a searchlight on it, and naturally, we don't spend our nights inspecting the car park with a searchlight.'

'What about the other buildings?'

'In effect there's only the City Hall. The fourth side of the park is bounded by blind ends and derelict property. We questioned the nightwatchman from the City Hall, but it appears that he was doing his pools in the basement.'

Gently was conscious of Stephens leaning forward from behind him. He turned his head. 'You've got a question, Inspector?'

'Yes, sir – if I may! Perhaps the Chief Inspector can tell me . . . I was wondering how chummie got the woman into the car park – that is to say, when she was waiting for her bus?'

It wasn't a question as much as an answer. Put like that, it immediately offered the solution. Gently nodded his satisfaction at his lieutenant's acuteness, and from the corner of his eye he noticed the youngster colouring up.

'Of course . . . !' Hansom could tell a hawk from a harnser. 'He was offering her a lift, that's as plain as my eye. He was someone who knew she was going to catch that bus home, and what's more, he was someone who was known to Shirley Johnson.'

'And had his car on the car park.'

'Too true . . . her husband! He was sculling around in his car all the evening. He says he was on a pub crawl out by Halford Ferry and Lordham, but it's a fact that we can't check his movements after half past nine.'

'It might equally well have been someone else . . .'

'Don't you believe it – Derek Johnson hated her guts. He's the dead spit of Neville Heath, eyes, curls and everything. I could smell him for our man the moment I set eyes on him, it was only this other business that put me off him for a bit.'

Gently shrugged indifferently, knowing Hansom's enthusiasms from of old. It needed only the appearance of progress to set him in full cry. But Stephens's suggestion, though it narrowed the field a little further, didn't point to Derek Johnson or to any other individual.

'Do you know where the Palette Group members parked their cars?'

Stephens had taken the question off Gently's lips.

'They're a poverty-stricken bunch, I shouldn't think they'd got any cars.'

'Not the chairman, St John Mallows?'

'Oh, him. *He*'s got a Daimler.'

'And did you find out where he parked it?'

'Huh . . . ! Hansom made a contemptuous motion of his head.

A moment later, however, he climbed off his high horse. He was far from being dense when he gave himself time to think.

'There are two or three others who own heaps of some sort – Aymas is one, and Farrer, and Allstanley. But I wouldn't mind betting that they parked them in the Haymarket – or Chapel Street, in front of us. That'd be nearest for the George III.'

'But, to date, you haven't made any definite inquiry?'

'Nope. I like to leave something for Scotland Yard to have a chew at.'

Gently smothered a grin in the lighting of his pipe. It hadn't taken Stephens long to measure swords with the handsome Hansom. Already, he was sure, the Chief Inspector bore a 'difficult' label – without being aware of it, he was supporting Northshire's reputation. And now, with hands that trembled slightly, Stephens was also lighting his pipe . . .

'Let's leave that for the moment. I'd like to hear more about the Johnsons. You haven't got a portrait of the victim, I suppose?'

Hansom dipped into the manilla folder which had contained the official photographs, finally selecting a half-plate print to skim across the desk to Gently.

'That's a recent one, I'm told . . . It just about gives the right effect. Don't forget that you're talking to an eyewitness – I danced with this femme, at the Charity Ball.'

He leaned his elbows on the desk and watched as Gently examined the print. It showed a fragile-looking blonde whose eyes, one could swear, had been hyacinth blue. The hair was short and only slightly wavy, the nose rather straight over a small mouth and chin. Though not very striking she'd been pretty in a way . . . for a moment, Gently couldn't put a name to the quality.

'You begin to catch on, do you? Well, you're wrong – she wasn't a lesbian. She'd got the look and the manner, but you only saw her around with men. Mind you, she might have had some girlfriends in private . . . that's possible: but she was the one and only female who belonged to the Palette Group.'

Gently inclined his head, passing the portrait on to Stephens.

'How old would she be?'

'Twenty-nine last May. She stood five feet seven and had a fashion-horse sort of figure – as lean as a lath, with just a top dressing of sex. She had a bedward way of gazing at you with her innocent blue eyes. Her voice was the tinkling sort, but you can bet it had an edge, too.'

'Did she belong to these parts?'

'Not her. They came from Bedford. Johnson arrived here five years ago and branched out as an estate agent.

He's a right Battle-of-Britain charlie, complete with MG. You could hang up your hat and coat on one side of his handlebars.'

'Does he make a go of the business?'

'His car and clothes say he does.'

'You've seen his flat, of course?'

'Yeah. It's a posh, brand new one. Over an office block.'

Hansom produced the estate agent's statement – not a great deal to show for three hours of grilling – and Gently skimmed through its inevitable police jargon, pausing occasionally for Stephens, who was reading over his shoulder.

A peculiar household must that one have been! Here and there, through the stiff formality, a telling phrase or two crept out. 'I wanted Shirley to have a baby but to this she would not agree.' 'I bought a new bed for the guest room and have been sleeping there for three years.' 'I do not know if she has been unfaithful and I myself have not been unfaithful.' 'I agree that I wanted a divorce, but that she would not contemplate a divorce.'

And then his account of Monday evening:

'When I arrived home my wife was going out. I did not ask her where she was going as we had agreed not to ask one another this. I found some eggs in the larder and poached two for my tea. Then I got out my car again and drove first to the Halford Ferry public house and afterwards to several public houses, including the Lordham Dog and the Porter Haynor Falgate. I returned to the Ferry and remained there till closing time, fetching my drinks from the bar to a table by the river. I arrived home at eleven o'clock or soon after. I went straight to bed without visiting my wife's room, and I did not know that she was missing until I was informed of it by the police.'

Hansom sneered: 'He was playing it close to the chest, don't you think? The innocent wronged husband who doesn't know a thing! We checked at the pubs which he condescended to mention, and like I told you, they don't remember him after half past nine.'

'Is he fairly well known to them?'

'You bet. He's that type. His MG would do the circuit with him blind drunk in the dickey.'

'Halford Ferry is that large pub . . . ?'

'Yep. He's a regular clever boyo. It's big, and rushed off its feet at this time of the year. Naturally, they won't swear that he wasn't there till closing, especially with him claiming that he sat at an outside table. He *may* have sat nursing a pint for an hour.'

'It's either true or very clever.'

'Cobber, you've put him in a nutshell.'

The Super, feeling perhaps that he was being ignored, now filled in some details of their investigation of Johnson. His service record was good, they knew nothing against his character, and though he owned a fast car his licence was virgin of endorsements. He had friends in his own profession and was generally well thought of. His business was honestly conducted and had a good reputation. That he was estranged from his wife was no secret to his acquaintances, but the subject was painful to him and he became abrupt if she was mentioned.

'Can anyone vouch for the time he arrived home?'

'No, and that and the time he gives seem to lend support to his good faith. If he had known at what time his wife

28

had been killed, he could have sworn that he was home by ten without fear of contradiction. Inspector Hansom here thinks that it's an example of Johnson's cunning, but failing evidence to the contrary one is bound to allow him the doubt. It was small things like these which made us uncertain about Johnson, and I suggested that we should turn our attention elsewhere.'

'Elsewhere', of course, was the Palette Group and its members, and from Hansom's bored expression Gently could judge what luck they had had. From his folder the local man produced a sheaf of bitty statements, the result of many hours of unprofitable labour.

'Perhaps you could give me the overall picture.'

'Sonny, I'd be delighted! They all had a "thing" about her.'

'Infatuation, you mean?'

'Hell, no – these are painters! There were some who thought she could paint, and the rest who thought she couldn't. Apart from some guessing about times, there's damn-all else.'

Gently paused for an instant before putting his next question; he wasn't confident that Hansom could give him the answer.

'Did it strike you as being the . . . usual relation, as between artists, or was there a little bit more of a point to it?'

'How the devil should I know!' Hansom stared his disgust at Gently. 'They're queers, the whole bunch, and that's putting it mildly. The fact that she was croaked didn't seem to have penetrated – they were only concerned with the way she lashed paint on.'

'But they were concerned about that – they held strong opinions?'

'I couldn't get them to talk about anything else. And yesterday it broke out again, when they opened the exhibition. We had to grab that picture to save ourselves a riot.'

The picture was produced and displayed on the top of a filing cabinet. On the whole, it seemed to lack something as a potential riot-raiser. A monotone drawing of about eighteen by twelve, it showed practised execution but no startling originality. There were qualities, however, which had been lost in reproduction. The figure wasn't striding through rain but through a grove of wire-like stalks. And it was a strangely evil figure, something medieval and witch-like; little breasts, like shrivelled gourds, hung from the wasted and wrinkled chest.

'Urs Graaf . . . possibly Dürer.'

Stephens, it appeared, was knowledgeable in art. Both the Super and Hansom viewed the picture with degrees of distaste.

'But that's the sort of thing she'd paint . . . !' Hansom lofted his beefy shoulders. 'She was dried up somewhere herself, with all her beautiful come-on eyes.'

'Have you seen her other pictures?'

'There's a room full of them, back at the flat. I saw a pair that hung in her bedroom, but I hadn't any reason to look at the rest.'

Oddly, though, the picture seemed to fascinate them, and each one kept his eyes fixed upon it. In the Super's office there was silence for a minute while they steadily appraised the dead woman's last conception.

'Their chairman . . . what had he to say about her painting?'

'Oh . . . him! Well, he was more sober than the rest. As a matter of fact, I don't think he mentioned it. It was from him that I managed to get the facts about the meeting.'

It had lasted three hours, from seven-thirty till ten-thirty. According to Mallows, it had run its usual course. The members, carrying their pictures, had foregathered in the cellar, and, aided by pints from up the stairs, had criticized each other's work.

'There was a little bit of business – subscriptions, reports, the usual thing. Then they started showing the pictures on an easel they'd fetched along. Mallows, being the chairman, was the first to have a crack, after which all present took a hand in the discussion. When they'd had a bellyful of one picture they set up another, and started crabbing that.'

'Did Mrs Johnson show a picture?'

'No, but she was a leading critic. Apparently she carried a bit of weight about the cellar. They would listen to her even when they were hotted up – because she was the only sheila there, do you think?'

Then followed the important timetable of the order in which the meeting broke up, though Hansom warned Gently that it wasn't unanimously subscribed to. Mallows had given him the outline and he had checked it with the various members, but some of them couldn't remember and others denied its accuracy.

What appeared was that six members had left the cellar before Mrs Johnson, one of them, Shoreby, as early as ten, in order to catch his last bus to Cheapham. The others had

31

left when the proceedings ended, all of them within two or three minutes of each other. Their names were Seymour, Lavery, Farrer, Baxter and Allstanley, but the precise order of their leaving could not be agreed on. Mallows thought that Allstanley was the first to depart, but Allstanley denied it and said that someone went out ahead of him. Lavery admitted that he was one of the first to leave the cellar, but claimed that he had returned to fetch his canvas, which he had forgotten.

'And after those six came Mallows and Mrs Johnson?'

'That's right. They stood in the doorway chatting for a moment. The cellar at the George III has got a separate door from the pub – it's on a little side-lane, at the end of the marketplace.'

'Then he saw her depart in the direction of the bus stop?'

'Yeah . . . that seems to indicate that his car was parked elsewhere.'

'Which makes him the last person to have seen Mrs Johnson alive.'

'Excepting everybody else she might have passed on her way.'

Along with the reports, that had to be enough for the present. The solemn boom of the City Hall clock had already announced the hour of lunch. Superintendent Walker, who had a great respect for his meals, had for the last five minutes been pointedly examining his wristwatch.

'Just one other thing – the knife. Did you find out where it was purchased?'

'They stock them at Carter Brown's, a draughtsman's supplier in Prince's Street.'

'But they don't remember selling this one?'

'Not on your life. That would make it too easy. They haven't sold one for several years – there's a plastic job which has swept the market.'

For lunch, Gently took Stephens to a café which he knew about in Glove Street. The young Inspector had little to say to him as he accompanied him thither. Until the sweet came he was silent, a picture of solemn preoccupation, then, dipping his spoon in a trifle, he murmured:

'It's got to be blackmail or nothing!'

Through a mouthful Gently murmured back:

'Unless the estate agent's got a girlfriend . . .'

CHAPTER THREE

IT MAY HAVE been that chance remark which led him first to visit Johnson's office, thus ignoring some obvious preliminaries which, quite frankly, ought to have been seen to. These included a visit to the dustbins, a step which Stephens regarded as de rigueur: Gently, with a better appreciation of Hansom, expected small profit from this piece of routine.

He had, moreover, used the car park in the past, and so was familiar with the general layout. More important for him, in the initial stages, were the things with which his mind's eye was unable to help him.

'I think I'll take a look at the husband! Perhaps you'd like to go back to HQ?'

'Whatever you say, sir. But shouldn't we, to start with—?'

'I'll leave that to you, then we won't be duplicating our efforts.'

Stephens, as he had intended, was mildly complimented by this, but a little to Gently's surprise the young man preferred to tag along with his senior.

'The husband, after all, is the number one suspect . . .'

It went without saying that Stephens was a graduate from Ryton. He was a product of the new policy for catching promising material young. He had been groomed into inspectorhood at an age when Gently had been proud to be a sergeant, and as with others of the new school, textbook lore came readily to his tongue.

Johnson's office was in Upper Queen Street, in the business area of the city. It was housed in a Victorian building which owned a dignified, sugar-ice front. The street was a traffic artery to the north and was busy with steady streams of vehicles; it adjoined the cathedral precincts at one end and was closed by the GPO at the other. The office had a prosperous appearance and it rejoiced in some brilliant paintwork. To air-force blue had been added crimson linings, with a touch of gilt on the scroll above the portal. On the plate-glass of the window appeared Johnson's name in discreet small capitals; the window was backed by a pegboard, to which details of the properties were attached.

'He seems to get the county people . . .' Gently brooded over the photographs and particulars. Very few of the advertised properties were at addresses in the city. A score or more of the neatly typed cards referred to substantial country houses, and there were mentions of shooting rights and 'half a mile of the best coarse fishing'. It was the sort of estate-agent's window before which Gently had often stood and dreamed.

The clerk's office behind the window developed this note of established prosperity. It was furnished in contemporary style and contained electric typewriters and the most modern equipment. Two of the typists were middle-aged women and they paid no attention to the intruders; but the third, a rather sharp-faced brunette, rose to greet them with a flashing smile.

'Is Mr Johnson busy at present?'

'Did you want to see him especially, sir?'

The smile went into a decline when Gently introduced himself, and the two typers, looking up quickly, showed that they could listen as they worked.

A handsomely carpeted flight of stairs took them up to the first floor. The receptionist flounced ahead of them, her spiked heels trotting briskly. By the time they had reached the landing Johnson had emerged from his room to meet them; another girl, carrying a shorthand note-book, slipped out of the room and went down the stairs.

'I saw they'd called you in, old sport!' Johnson was insisting on shaking their hands. 'They plastered it over the local, you know, and me, with a gendarme's hand on my shoulder . . .'

He was so much to type that it was difficult to believe in him – you felt he must be clowning it, laying it on a bit. But there wasn't much that was funny in the tone of his voice, and after the first defiant stare, his eyes switched about him nervously.

'Come into the ops room . . .'

He turned and preceded them into his office, which in its smartness was of a piece with the rest of the premises. With an attempt at an air he swaggered across to his desk, and before sprawling into the revolving chair, spun it once with his fingertip.

'I always do that – it's a gimmick I've got.'

'Something you picked up in the Service?'

Johnson nodded his head briskly. 'I used to do it in the mess before we took off on a prang . . . then one day I forgot, and copped a packet over Cologne. Bloody Lanc went up in smoke. Mine was the only chute that opened. Funny thing, wasn't it, cocker? All the way down I was laughing my head off . . .'

His grey eyes fastened for an instant on Gently's, as though watchfully seeking the Yard man's reaction. It produced an unpleasant impression, a feeling of distrust. What had Hansom said about Johnson? 'I could smell him for our man . . .'

Hansom had also said that Johnson resembled Heath, but perhaps he was judging from the press photograph of the murderer. Certainly they both had fair wavy hair, and eyes of pale grey that stared a little. But Johnson's features were heavier and broader, he lacked the cleft chin and the length of the nose. His mouth, too, was stronger, a mouth full of determination. It looked as though it knew how to keep itself shut.

'You've come here to put me through it again? It's like the old days with the Gestapo, cocker. Don't apologize or anything – I'm well up in the drill. I've been through worse grillings than you'll ever dish out.'

'This is just a routine recap, Mr Johnson.'

'Good show! I love going through it ten times.'

'I'm hoping that so much repetition won't be necessary.'

Gently pulled up one of the office's plastic-seated iron chairs. At a respectful distance, Stephens also took a seat. Johnson had shaken a cigarette from a torn-open packet, and having struck a match on his nail, was puffing smoke out noisily.

37

'You knew that your wife was a member of the Palette Group, Mr Johnson?'

'That's a silly question, cocker. I couldn't very well not know it.'

'How long had she been a member?'

'Two years or thereabouts. But she'd always mucked about with paints, even before we got hitched up.'

'So for two years she had attended their meetings?'

'Roger. And I knew about it all the time.'

'You knew that they met on the first Monday of each month?'

'And that the meetings lasted from half-seven to half-ten.'

'I just wanted to get that clear, Mr Johnson. In your statement you merely said that you didn't ask her where she was going.'

'Whizzo. I thought you were leading up to something!'

'Naturally, I wanted to establish that you knew where and when to find her.'

The smoke hissed through Johnson's teeth but he made no comment. He was tilting his chair backwards and had got his chin buried in his pullover. Though Gently had purposely sat to his side, the estate agent was facing ahead so that he avoided the light from the window.

'You've got a useful set of reference books in your office, Mr Johnson . . .'

Again there was no comment except the fierce expulsion of some smoke. He had a peculiar way of doing it, it was like the growling of a dog; the smoke emerged in an upward fan between the two horns of his massive moustache.

'The current Kelly's . . . is that a Blomefield? . . . and surely a run of Ladbrooke's *Churches*. And an estate agent like yourself should have a fairish selection of maps . . .'

Johnson slid open a drawer of his desk and pulled out a mint-looking Ordnance Survey map. He weighed it for a second in his hand, and then adroitly copped it to Gently.

'You can drop all the crafty stuff straight away, cocker. I tell you, I'm used to interrogation by experts. I've had three thousand and ten official lectures on security – plus the pleasure of being put through the mill by the Nazis.'

Gently shrugged, examining the map that Johnson had tossed him. It was indeed new, but bore a typed label on its cover:

'Route taken by Derek Johnson on Monday, 5 July, with approximate times and number of pints imbibed.'

Inside the route was marked in heavy green ink: it corresponded exactly to what Johnson had given in his statement.

'When did you cook this up?'

'After the locals started in on me.'

'For your benefit or theirs?'

'Mine of course – don't be naive.'

'You know that it doesn't give you an alibi for the murder?'

'A bloody shame, isn't it? But that's my story, and sticking to it.'

Gently nodded his head slowly and with a little reluctant admiration. He was beginning to understand why Hansom had had his doubts about Johnson. The man possessed a certain panache, a degree of bold and persuasive frankness. One could set a query against it, but on the balance, felt inclined to accept it.

'Why did you move up here from Bedford?'

There was another thing, too, concerning Johnson. The case against him rested entirely on suspicion, it didn't admit of any pressure or of trapping by contradiction. With no alibi to support, he had no worthwhile handle to him.

'Not to murder my wife, you can bet your shirt on that. I was looking for a business, and there was one up here for sale. I didn't pinch my capital either – it was left me by my mother. As for the district, I've always liked it – I was stationed up here for most of the war.'

'Is it a good one for the business?'

'It depends on what you handle. Being outside the commuting range, the properties here are relatively cheap. So I look for customers down south who want more consequence than they can afford in Surrey. A four-bedroom man down there can usually rise to eight in Northshire.'

'You deal mostly in country properties?'

'Roger. I specialize in them.'

'Do you have any difficulty in finding them?'

'Why the hell should I? There's plenty about.'

For an instant it seemed to Gently that Johnson was uneasy, and he deliberately paused to see if anything would develop. But the silence produced nothing except some more hissing smoke, and then the replacement of the first cigarette by a second.

'You yourself prefer to live in the city, however?'

Was he imagining it, or had he really touched something?

'Why not? I was born and bred in a town. There have never been any swede-bashers in our line of the family.'

'And your wife felt the same way?'

'No she didn't, as a matter of fact. Since you're curious, I had some thoughts of moving out of the city. Not that it would have made a scrap of difference – things had gone too far for that. But a flat's a small place when you get on each other's wick.'

'You'd actually settled on a place?'

This time it was Johnson who made the pause. For several seconds he fanned out smoke before he decided on a reply.

'No, I hadn't, suppose it matters. I was still looking round for one. Being an estate agent and all that, one doesn't rush into properties quickly.'

'Was your wife very insistent about it?'

'No. You can lay off sniping round that. My wife had given up being insistent about anything – except ignoring her husband's existence.'

Gently stared at the map, which was still unfolded over his knees. His instinct assured him that they were on a very interesting subject. He explored it for a little, trying to see if he could tie it in, but it involved him in hypotheses of which the facts gave no suggestion. First catch your fact . . .

He sighed and returned to Johnson.

'Your wife was younger than you, I believe?'

'You know she was if you read my statement.'

'Seven years, I believe it was.'

'Let's be precise – seven years and two months.'

'Where did you meet your wife, Mr Johnson?'

'In Bedford. She was my boss's secretary. When I came out of the airworks I took a job with Wright and McOubrey – they're estate agents in the town. I went there to learn the business.'

41

'She had relatives in Bedford, of course?'

'Her father. He died two years ago. Then there's a cousin who lives in Evesham. That's the lot, as far as I know.'

'Did you ever meet the cousin?'

'Only once, when he came to the wedding. He's a thin and miserable type, he manages a canning factory over there. I sent him a note with the time of the funeral – that was yesterday – but he didn't turn up.'

The phone rang on his desk and Johnson scooped it to his ear. In the clerk's office below a customer was apparently asking for him. He listened for half a minute, his eyes fixed in front of him, then he barked out some instructions and slammed the phone back on its rest.

The object his eyes had been fixed upon was a small ivory paper knife. It was yellowed, as though by sunlight, and a little serrated at the edges.

'Where was it we got to . . . ?'

His eyes flashed at Gently aggressively. Then, as they had done at first, they wandered away and about the room. He lit a third cigarette from the butt of the second, grinding the latter out with emphasis in a tray which bore the RAF crest.

'We'd got to where you met your wife in Bedford.'

'Roger. It's a day I shan't forget in a hurry. She came as a temporary when McOubrey's secretary was sick, but she only left it to marry me – she was a sticker, was dear Shirley.'

'You thought differently, then, I take it?'

'I'm not so blazing sure of that. Ask any second man how he came to be married, and if he's honest, he won't

42

be able to tell you. She wasn't my type of female at all. She was lean and blonde and a bit of a pansy. She used a rank sort of scent which I loathed the smell of – like poppies and horse piss, if you can imagine the combination. Well, I suppose she had her eye on me, that's the way it usually happens. It gratified my vanity and I used to take her out. We went to dances and the flicks, and home to meet her papa, and before you could say "bingo" I was standing at the altar.

'Believe me, cocker, it's still a bit of a surprise packet. I've never quite been able to see myself as her husband.'

Johnson inhaled long puffs and fizzed them out at the ceiling – he really did sound surprised at this strange thing which life had done to him. A picture passed through Gently's mind of a younger, callower Johnson, a Johnson in his Service uniform, drinking pints with his mates in the local. At twenty-one he had commanded a bomber. At twenty-two, been shot out of the sky. And then, settling down at last to build a life, he'd fallen into the hands of the husband-hunting Shirley.

Strong meat for the prosecution . . . even stronger for the defence!

'How many years had you been married?'

'It would have been seven in September. At first I rented a house at Kimbolton, then I bought one on the Goldington road. Her papa used to live at Goldington. He was a dry old stick who raised prize chrysanthemums.'

'Did you used to get on, at first?'

'It depends what you mean by "get on", cocker.'

'Was the marriage consummated?'

'Good show! Oh yes, it was. I want to give Shirley her

due – she put on a pretty good act, to begin with. You couldn't accuse her of being enthusiastic, but she gritted her teeth and went ahead with the exercise.'

'Would you describe her as being frigid?'

'It's a funny thing, but I can't answer that. As far as I was concerned she was frigid enough, but I always had the impression that there might have been more to her.'

'What gave you that impression?'

'Sorry, cocker. Don't know.'

'Was she friendly with other men?'

'Not to the extent of going to bed with them.'

'And what about women?'

'Aha.' Johnson looked knowing. 'I've had my doubts about that, but I could never nail her down. She had some girlfriends back at Bedford who I wouldn't have trusted far, but I've got no positive evidence. It could be my filthy mind.'

'Was there anything like that up here?'

Johnson slowly shook his head.

'For the last three years I haven't kept an eye on her, we've slept in separate rooms, eaten apart, avoided each other. She could have gone to the devil for all I'd have known about it, though to be fair, I never heard any scandal regarding her. About the last thing we did together was to bury her father. She took on a bit then, and it seemed we might be going to start afresh. But it only lasted a week, and then things were worse than ever; it seemed to set a seal on it, cocker. After that there was no going back.'

'Didn't it occur to either of you to get a divorce?'

'Too true it did – it occurred to me.'

'You suggested it to her?'

'I offered to give her the grounds for it. Only Shirley wasn't the type to let a husband off the hook.'

From his chair near a filing cabinet Stephens was trying to catch his senior's eye. In his urgent, jiffling impatience he reminded Gently of a schoolboy.

'Inspector Stephens has something to ask you.'

Stephens was actually clearing his throat! Johnson, breathing out smoke like a grampus, half turned to appraise this threat on his flank.

'Fire away.'

'It's about the Palette Group . . . I suppose you never attended a meeting?'

'Di-dah-di-dah!' Johnson grimaced his contempt. 'Do I look the sort of bloke who would hold hands with that lot?'

'I was wondering if you were acquainted with any of the members.'

'As it happens I am, though only in the way of business. My bank manager fancies himself as an artist, and I sold a piece of property for their chairman, St John Mallows.'

'A piece of property! When would that have been?'

'Does it matter, or something? I sold it in January.'

Stephens's dark eyes were gleaming and he had edged his chair forward. His next question was rapped out in Superintendental style:

'Did your wife introduce him to you?'

'Did she firkin! He came through the bank. He asked Farrer to recommend him an agent, and Farrer put him on to me.'

'The property – it was valuable?'

'A couple of cottages out Herling way. The rents didn't

cover the outgoings on them, and my commission on the sale only just squared the advertising.'

'Did your wife ever mention St John Mallows to you?'

'I thought I'd made it plain that we didn't exchange small talk.'

'Now about her estate, sir. Was it around what you expected?'

'Yes – the proceeds from her papa's house, plus a hundred or so which she'd saved from her allowance.'

It was all rather discouraging, and Stephens couldn't help looking crestfallen. To make it worse, Johnson was watching him with a sort of quizzical amusement. To cover his embarrassment the young Inspector pulled out his pipe; but even this chanced to be unemptied, and he was reduced to sucking it cold.

'And those are the only members of the Group with whom you are personally acquainted . . . ?'

Johnson returned his attention to the other side of the room.

'I said so, didn't I? Actually, they belong to the same golf club . . . I may have seen some of the others, but I've never met them to talk to.'

'So you can't tell us anything about your wife's relations with them?'

'Not a sausage, old sport. She might have gone to bed with the lot of them.'

Gently folded the map and stowed it in one of his pockets.

'Are you busy this afternoon? . . . I'd like to see over your wife's belongings.'

★ ★ ★

46

Johnson drove them there himself in his snarling red MG — a car that fascinated Gently, fresh from his somewhat *passé* Riley. It was a luscious piece of machinery, sharp with response and explosive power. Johnson, driving it with his fingertips, moved up through the traffic with a surgeon-like precision. Surely, now that one was a Super, and on the Metropolitan scale . . . ?

The flat was situated in Baker's Court, a short cul-de-sac off Viscount Road. As Hansom had told them, it was an area of office blocks, and the flat itself surmounted the branch of an insurance firm. Cars were parked in relays on all sides of the court, and office workers kept up a perpetual coming and going. Through a dozen or more of the wide-open windows one could hear the clicking and tinkle of hard-worked typewriters.

'The beauty of this place is that it's quiet at night . . .'

Having squeezed in his car, Johnson conducted them across the court. Beside a blue-painted door was a framed card which bore his name, while on the door, with tips elevated, was screwed a chromium-plated horseshoe.

'Another relic of the Service?'

'Roger! . . . Got to keep the gremlins out.'

In the act of unlocking the door, he paused to finger the token of luck. At the top of the stairway inside they passed a Spitfire, poised on a pedestal, and this also he managed to touch, though with a sudden, furtive motion.

All in all Gently found the flat disappointing, though why it would have been difficult for him to say. He had not been expecting to make any grand discovery, coming three days late in the footsteps of Hansom. The victim's belongings had already been checked. A few bits of correspondence had been collected and read. There was a gloomy neatness in the rooms she had occupied, as though everything there had been pondered and put away.

'Where did she used to do her painting?'

The pictures he soon grew tired of examining. They were monotones from beginning to end, all vaguely allegorical and in some way distasteful. A number of them were on phallic themes, and one or two were plainly sexual fantasies. Her behaviour towards Johnson may have suggested frigidity, but there had been no fetters on her flights of imagination.

'She used to paint here in the bedroom, cocker.'

'I wouldn't have thought the light would have been very suitable.'

'It didn't matter a damn – she used to paint at night. I've seen the light under her door as late as two or three in the morning.'

'How did you know that she was painting?'

'You could smell it, that's how. The place used to reek of turpentine and linseed. And you could hear her, too, when she was using a big brush – and there'd be her clutter of things in the sink in the morning.'

Pipe in mouth, Gently strolled to the metal-framed window, which looked down on some mews to the rear of the building. Beneath it, to the ground, stretched a smooth wall of glazed brick: the cream paint on the sill was in part worn and marked. He turned on his heel.

'She had a door key, of course?'

'That's right – she didn't need to go out through the window.'

'Did you think that she might have?'

'Not till a moment ago. But I'm not quite as dumb as I look, old sport.'

Gently nodded indefinitely and puffed once or twice. He had suddenly noticed that Johnson was sweating. For a second or two he seemed on the verge of a fresh question, then he motioned to Stephens, and picked up his hat.

CHAPTER FOUR

A LAZY BREEZE tempered the warm afternoon, and Gently, ignoring the buses, elected to walk back along Viscount Road. He was suddenly in a mood for the early summer weather: it seemed exactly to suit his contemplative frame of mind.

Once more he had embarked on a case that intrigued him. During those last few moments with Johnson, he had felt the surge of the mysterious current. From being a collection of dead facts the case had sprung into vibrant life, he was getting it into his hands, beginning to sense a possible shape. Perhaps never before had he so relished the exercising of his powers. His spell of duty in the metropolis had done that for him, at least. In another way it had been a tall milestone in his career: it had pulled him up, made him see himself, confirmed the talent that was his . . .

'Don't you think, sir, that we can safely rule Johnson out of it?'

He had hardly been aware of Stephens, striding smartly along beside him. The sudden clarity of vision which his mood had induced had been extending itself to the busy world passing about him. This city had always been the home of painters . . . at last, he thought he had hit on one of the reasons. There was a quality in the light here, a steady, glowing luminosity. Was it due to the dry, continental east wind?

'I don't know what your impressions were, sir, but I rather had the feeling that he was on the up-and-up. I admit that he struck me as being a little calculating, but I don't think that one should be too influenced by that.'

'What do you mean by being calculating?'

Gently mentally shrugged his shoulders – how these youngsters tried to reduce everything to an immaculate black and white!

'Well, sir, he was making the best of his case. I think you'll agree with me about that. He set himself to sound convincing by pretending to have nothing to hide.'

'And you think that he succeeded?'

'Quite frankly, sir, I do. He made a number of risky admissions which he might just as well have kept in the bag.'

'Like his knowledge of the Group meeting?'

'Yes, sir, particularly that. There was no need for him to have stuck his neck out so far. I realize that in theory it might be put down to cleverness, but in practice, sir, did you ever meet with cleverness of that kind?'

Gently grudgingly admitted it. 'Only in defence counsels . . . ! When your own neck is at stake, you don't set puzzles of that kind. All the same, it would have been odd if he hadn't known about the meeting.'

'On the balance, sir, I think you must allow it's in his favour.'

Which was to echo the shrewd Superintendent Walker, of course, not to mention handsome Hansom's more rhapsodical judgements. Johnson had it in the balance: that was the general conclusion, though Hansom was inclined to give the scales a prejudiced nudge.

'One can't always strike a balance . . .'

Here, again, he was making a discovery – he, in his approach to a case, had never drawn up accounts of this kind. They were a compromise with the truth and he had automatically distrusted them; his way was to assemble the facts and to hold them suspended in his mind, where, by a sort of alchemy, they eventually moved into a pattern.

'Yes, sir, I agree. But one has to have a shot at it.'

'It's a process which is liable to error, Stephens.'

'But you've got to have some method for treating the facts, sir.'

'If you can see the facts clearly, there's no need for a method.'

He could see he was puzzling Stephens, and suddenly he smiled at him paternally. He knew that it was no use trying to explain himself to the young man. It would take long years of experience, of persistent trial and error, before Stephens came to accept that detection was an art and not a science. Even Gently, at the top of his tree, had only just begun to see that . . .

'We'll take a look at the exhibition before we return to HQ. It'll give us something to chat about when we put the painters through it.'

The way to the Castle Gardens, however, took them past the City Hall and its car park, and Gently hadn't the heart to head his colleague off them again. As usual at that hour, the park was jam-packed with lines of vehicles. An elderly attendant in a navy-blue uniform was doing his best to produce a semblance of order.

'Superintendent Gently, CID. Are those the dustbins where the police found the body?'

This was also for Stephens's benefit, since Gently could identify the site from the photographs. There were six of them standing in a well-dragooned row, heavy-quality, galvanized Corporation dustbins; than these it would have been hard to imagine a more innocent sequence of useful ironware. Nothing remained to suggest that a tragedy had been enacted. All traces of blood had been carefully erased. The terrace wall, against which the dustbins were ranged, marked the boundary of HQ's section of the park.

'He was a cheeky sort of chummie, sir . . . when you come to weigh it up!'

Gently nodded his agreement, his eye running round the open space. It was largely contained by the interior angle which was formed by the backs of the City Hall and Police HQ. Opposite to the City Hall were the blind ends and a brick wall, beside which ran a footway joining Chapel Street with St Saviour's. The last-mentioned street made the fourth side of the square; it faced the car park with a number of small shops, and a lane.

'It couldn't have been altogether dark over here.'

Stephens was hard at it studying the angles of the site. Above it all, sanctifying the spot with civic dignity, rose the great tower of the City Hall with its clock face of gilt studs.

'By half past ten . . . at this time of the year . . .'

'I seem to remember that it was cloudy on Monday.'

'All the same, there's three lamps in the street over there, and a small one on the wall where you go out past HQ.'

Stephens paused to eye the police building with a touch of malevolence – this was certainly an unfortunate spot for a murder! There were about twenty yards, if it came to hard figures, which separated the dustbins from the windows of the canteen. But then, even police canteens ran to curtains.

'Under the circumstances it could scarcely have been premeditated. Nobody but an idiot would plan a murder right here. Having got her here, he must have acted on impulse – he might have been carrying that paper knife in the locker of his car.'

'Then you think it was bona fide, his offer of a lift?'

'Well, sir, he might have planned to do it somewhere else. But then finding that it was quiet here, temptation got the better of him. He may have done it in his car – we might be able to find the traces.'

It was plain enough that Stephens was chafing for a bit of action. Unlike Dutt, he wasn't used to Gently's seeming-casual ways. The murderer would have had three days in which to clean or not clean his car, but the urgency of beginning a check sounded keenly in Stephens's voice.

'All right . . . cut along to Hansom and see if we can get those cars pulled in. Though I would like to have talked to the drivers before you started to put the wind up them.'

'I don't want to upset your plans, sir—'

'That's all right. You may be lucky. And don't forget our friend Johnson's MG – I'd put that right at the head of the list.'

He chuckled as Stephens went striding away – another improbability had just occurred to him. Unless the murderer had happened to be left-handed, then he could hardly have done that job in his car. But the young Inspector wanted to be up and doing, and checking the cars was a chore which would have to be done. It might also do him good to work with Hansom for a spell . . . as an educating influence, the Chief Inspector had his points. Still chuckling, Gently continued on his way to the Castle Gardens.

There he had a stroke of luck, though it had not been unanticipated: he found the Palette Group's illustrious chairman busy lionizing in the Gardens. With his natural flair for publicity he was exploiting the moment's sensation, and long before Gently caught a glimpse of him he could hear the pontificating voice.

'Art for art's sake . . . that's the purest piece of moonshine! So is Lawrence's asinine assertion . . . doesn't bear inspection for a moment. If art was for *his* sake, then why did he bother to publish? Why didn't he burn his manuscript the moment after he'd finished scribbling . . . ?

'No, there is nothing here that will describe the creative process. Those who view art from a selfish standpoint haven't learnt their A B C . . .'

Characteristically, Mallows was expounding his artistic credo, the man himself almost lost to sight in the centre of his knot of admirers. It was the first time that Gently had seen the great man in the flesh, though pictures of him were commonplace in the papers and illustrated weeklies. According to your viewpoint he was a Philistine or a prophet. Of later years opinion had been swinging more towards the latter role.

'The first lesson in art is that art is a transitive term. It is a communication that takes place between one person and his fellows. The artist has a vision, a revelation of the truth, and this he needs to express, not to himself, but to other people . . .'

To get a better view of him, Gently climbed a few steps up the Mound. Mallows had a short and stocky figure which was easily hidden in a crowd. His features were thick and rather coarsened, but from a distance, very distinguished; he had a lavish head of iron-grey hair, locks of which were heaped over his forehead.

'In art, one distinguishes three pillars . . .'

His audience, Gently noticed, was largely of women. They were mostly well dressed in the provincial way, and hung upon every word he was uttering. Some of them were young, dressed in jeans and sloppy jumpers, and these were probably students from the flourishing Art School. But the majority were serious, middle-aged women, or women arrived at a certain age.

On the outskirts of the group stood one or two men with bored expressions. They stared about them while Mallows was talking, and stole occasional looks at the exhibits. These, displayed on scaffolds beneath canvas awnings, were being well patronized by a steady stream of viewers. The group of stands stood in a crescent along the foot of the steep Mound, shaded partly by the giant elms which were rooted in the bank above.

'These pillars are Vision, Expression and Reception. For the past fifty years or so the last pillar has been forgotten. The artists grew proud, they broke the law that gave them being. As a result we have witnessed anarchy, sterility and decadence, and an impudent arraignment of the public with whom the artists had broken faith . . .'

This was the doctrine which Mallows had been hammering for the last three decades, the doctrine that art was for someone, or that else it wasn't art. In the late twenties and early thirties it had raised storms of abuse and mockery, but as aesthetic mysticism had begun to decline, so had the storms died away to murmuring. A little, perhaps, of the truth had been with this upstart provincial shake-canvas . . .

But now Mallows had said his piece and was stalking across to the attendant's booth, leaving to break out behind him a cooing and animated conversation. Gently climbed down the steps again and also made his way to the booth. With the young man who sat at the table, Mallows was checking the sales of the pictures.

'May I have a word with you, sir . . . ?'

A pair of fierce grey-blue eyes rose to stare into his. Mallows had thick, up-brushed eyebrows ending in Mephistophelian points, and his jaw, one noticed, had an uncompromising jut to it.

'Damn it, you're not a reporter, are you?'

Gently modestly presented his credentials.

'Aha – so you're a policeman! I thought you had the professional approach. Now what can I do for you – do you want to buy a picture?'

'As yet, I haven't seen them—'

'Well, we'll soon take care of that. Nobody gets away from here without exposing themselves to our talent – put your notebook away, my dear fellow. You'd better come along with me.'

It was a novel situation, being required to 'go along with' someone, and Mallows supplied additional point to it by grasping Gently's arm. He led him past the first few stands, at which a number of people were clustered, and steered him into a booth in which were displayed some quaint fish pictures.

'There you are – what do you think of these? I read in the paper that you were an angler.'

Gently wondered whether to be frank and decided that he might as well be.

'They aren't the sort of fish I catch.'

'Ah! You're another one who doesn't like Wimbush. And yet the poor fellow keeps painting these fish, as though they were the be-all and end-all of life. Do you think he's a bit of a case?'

'I don't know . . . perhaps angling would help him.'

'Now you disappoint me, Superintendent. I was hoping you would quote me a snatch of Freud.'

Mallows quizzed him for a few moments from the depths of his five feet seven; then he darted a look round the booth, to establish the non-proximity of Wimbush lovers.

'Now – what do you want to see me about?'

'First, a question about your car . . .'

'It's a 1957 Daimler.'

'Where did you park it on Monday night, sir?'

'Hum.' Mallows cocked an eyebrow at him. 'Now it's really come to business, hasn't it? I suppose that if I'd parked it by a certain set of dustbins, you'd pull a rope out of your pocket and hang me from the next tree.'

'Did you park it there, then?'

'No, no, not I! In any case, you wouldn't park a Daimler by the dustbins.'

'Then where did you park it, sir?'

'On the Haymarket, as always. And since you're not going to believe me, I've got a witness who will prove it.'

His witness, it turned out, was an old-age pensioner, a self-appointed attendant at the Haymarket parking space. In return for small tips he kept an eye on the cars, and had some undisclosed method for keeping places for his regulars.

'Old George'll see me clear without applying for habeas corpus – unless you hold that I bribe him when I buy him a drink. And he'll vouch for Farrer too – he's another contributory parker – and Farrer and I will vouch for each other. What are you going to do about that?'

'Did any of the others park in the Haymarket?'

'The whole lot did, for all I know. But seriously, there are only one or two who aspire to cars – three, I think, beside me and Farrer. Only they aren't regulars at the Haymarket park, and so they'll have to supply their own guarantors.'

'Gould you give me their names?'

'If you promise them a fair trial. They are Baxter, Aymas and Allstanley, the bent-wire merchant. Baxter has got a Singer and Aymas an old Triumph. Allstanley is respectable – he's got a post-war Austin.'

'And none of them were parked in the Haymarket that evening?'

'I told you, I don't know. I was one of the first there.'

'But you know their cars – you'd have seen them there before?'

'Oh yes. It's the usual park for the Palette Group members.'

Of those three names, only one could be partly eliminated – Aymas's; he had left the cellar later than Mrs Johnson. It didn't put him in the clear, since he might have followed straight after her, but it made him a little less vulnerable than the others.

'I think you told Inspector Hansom that Allstanley was the first to leave – apart from Shoreby, of course, who went early to catch a bus?'

'That was what I dug up for him after racking my brains over it. But you know as well as I that such impressions are undependable.'

'You mean that you want to withdraw it?'

Mallows made a comical face at him. 'Come off it, my dear fellow, and let's discuss it like fellow mortals. I'm the chairman of that group, which means that I do a lot of talking. It's my business to open the proceedings, to keep them civil and to wind them up. And that, I assure you, is not a sinecure – if you think it is, you know little about painters.

'They're like a lot of bear-cats thrown together in a pit. I sometimes think that lion tamers have a softer job than I have. As a result, I don't have much time to tabulate arrivals and departures – when it's getting to half past ten, I'm busy trying to break them up. I know that Shoreby went for his bus and that Allstanley took his exit promptly; but if he says that someone left ahead of him, well, I wouldn't like to call him a liar.'

Gently nodded without enthusiasm, his eye on one of the fish pictures. Behind them, in the afternoon sunlight, people moved leisurely against a background of flowers.

'What can you tell me about this Allstanley?'

'He's picked up with wire. Which I think is a pity.'

'About his character, I mean.'

'Apart from that, I know nothing against him. He's just on forty and about my height – a lot of great men are five feet seven. He's a teacher and lives and works at Walford – that's a village some seven or eight miles out of town. He used to sculpt in beech before he got the wire bug. He's been with us now . . . oh, four or five years.'

'One of your bear-cats, is he?'

'Good heavens no. He's one of the quiet ones. Being a sculptor, perhaps, he feels aloof from the squalid mob.'

'A married man?'

'No. He runs a car, as I said. You can't have it all ways when you're merely a teacher.'

'Was he a friend of Mrs Johnson's?'

'Ah, now we come to the kernel . . . ! But we all had an eye on that lady, you know. She was a very popular member, a species of uncrowned royalty; and if it comes to that, I've taken her out to lunch myself.'

'But he was a friend, was he?'

'All right. He was.'

'Something more than a friend?'

'No, laddie. Just friendly.'

'On lunching terms, for instance?'

Mallows winked at him broadly. 'Even here, it isn't sinful to take a lady into Lyons.'

It was a gentle rebuke, and Gently acknowledged it with a shrug. Mallows wasn't going to be edged into tendentious guesses. Instead of trying further, Gently switched to

Baxter and Aymas, listening absently and with few questions as Mallows described them to him.

'Baxter is fortyish too, a lean fellow with an Adam's apple. He's principally a commercial artist and works in the art department of Hallman's. He whiffs at a silly little pipe and has a wicked tongue when he likes – actually, he's quite a good man. He's got a natural flair for poster colour.

'Aymas is younger than him, and quite a different brand of coffee. An angry young man, you'd probably call him, though you could substitute "ignorant" for "angry". He looks like, and is, a farm worker who has taught himself to paint. He's one of my principal bear-cats and I'm perpetually having to sit on him.

'Baxter is married and has three children, Aymas would like to be thought a Don Juan. He was as thick as anyone with Shirley – she'd got the refinement he admired, you understand. But I doubt if it went any further. Shirley was amused but she wasn't attracted. As for Aymas, he was satisfied to be thought her favourite – he basked, you might say, in her reflected culture. Incidentally, I left him arguing the toss in the cellar.'

'That brings me to another thing I wanted to ask you.'

Gently, at long last, had seen enough of the Wimbush fishes. They were curiously bloated and heavy-looking creatures, and though distinguished in detail, still depressingly alike.

'The meeting itself – can't you tell me something about that?'

'Tell you what, my dear fellow?'

'Wasn't it noisier than usual?'

Mallows screwed up his mouth. 'N-no, I wouldn't have said so. Just the same old fiddles playing the same old tunes.'

'And what tunes were they?'

Mallows twisted his mouth again; then he peered up at Gently, half questioning, half amused.

'To kick off with, you'd better have a look at the pictures. They'll probably tell you as much as I can about it. I'll just say this . . . they're a pretty fair sample. So have a look round, and then tell me what you find.'

This was something which Gently had intended doing in any case, and after a moment's silence, he fell in with the suggestion. With Mallows bobbing at his elbow he proceeded from stand to stand, answering with monosyllables and grunts the academician's exclamations.

Overall, it was such a mixture as one would have expected to find there, giving the impression of talent fixed between mediocrity and ability. Here and there a picture stood out as though in promise of better things, but one felt, in those surroundings, that such a picture was a lucky hit. There was nowhere to be seen the confident vitality of an established professional.

Every exhibit, in fact, seemed in the nature of an experiment, and gave no suggestion of powers of reproduction. After a number of failures a fortunate canvas had evolved, but one could sense the inability to command such another. Once a year, there would be one or two to put in the exhibition.

There was, however, a variety in the scope of the experiments, and this prevented the exhibition from being entirely dull. Apart from Wimbush's fish there were other unusual lines – Shoreby, for instance, painted geometrical panels, and Lavery postcard-size abstracts.

'That's Aymas's rude, raw brush . . .'

Mallows pointed to a group of three vigorous landscapes. They commanded a certain distinction by their daring use of primaries, but otherwise Gently could see in them little of interest.

'And yet the fellow has talent, if he ever lets it out. But he won't while he sticks to understudying Seago ... There's one of Baxter's posters – a surprising use of purple! – and a Phil Watts interior. He's the youngster at the desk.'

At the end of the tour Mallows turned to Gently expectantly, his brushed-up eyebrows giving him an owlish appearance.

'Did you get what I meant, or would you like me to tell you ... ?'

Gently grinned. 'I think I got it ... aren't there two schools of thought?'

'Splendid, splendid!' Mallows patted him on the shoulder. 'My opinion of you was never higher, Superintendent. You've hit the target first go – we've got a split down our middle. It's tradition versus modernism that rocks the cellar walls.'

'Aymas, Seymour and that lot ...'

'Precisely. Aymas is their champion.'

'Wimbush, Lavery and Shoreby—'

'They're the shock troopers of the opposition. Numerically, Superintendent, the two factions are about the same, but the reactionaries shout the louder and the opposition is the more biting.'

'And your job is to hold the balance?'

'That, alack, is my leading function. On the first Monday of every month I fetch my armour from the cupboard.'

Insensibly they had drawn back towards the booth of

Wimbush fishes, which continued the least frequented site of the exhibition. But now, Gently noticed, they had a periphery of followers – the bored characters, undoubtedly members, who had been listening to Mallows's address.

In reality there were but three of them, and they kept out of normal earshot; but they were persistent in their presence and their covert observation. Two of them kept together and exchanged occasional words. The third, a narrow-featured man, stood a little distance further off.

'Was it this split that caused the row . . . the one you had at the opening, yesterday?'

'What else, my dear fellow? It was a deplorable piece of business.'

'But it centred, I believe, on Mrs Johnson's exhibit?'

'That was only the spark which ignited the gunpowder.'

Was there a suspicion of briskness in Mallows's reply? Gently borrowed a moment while he felt for his pipe and tobacco. The RA, hands clasped behind him, appeared to be reassessing the Wimbush pictures; he had struck an attitude, his feet apart, his head thrust forward towards the canvases.

'In fact, where did Mrs Johnson fit into this set-up – did she side with tradition or was she one of the modernists?'

'Frankly, Superintendent – have you looked through her pictures?'

'I have, but they didn't answer the question for me.'

'There you are, then!' Mallows straightened up with a little spring. 'For my money, you're a pretty fair judge of these things. And I'm in the same position. I wouldn't like to try to classify her. Her method was certainly traditional, though her pictures were rank with symbolism.'

'Yet she must have taken a side . . . ?'

'No more she did than did her pictures. She had a talent for sitting on the fence, Superintendent. She was *persona grata* with both their houses. She could lean in both directions at once. She was an artist doubly committed, and both the factions would have claimed her.'

'And after her death they would come to blows about it?'

Mallows shrugged. 'That's a reasonable theory.'

'One you know to be a fact?'

'Damnation, Superintendent! I'm not a policeman.'

Suddenly the artist looked about him, seeming, for the first time, to notice their following. He emitted a short, explosive 'Hah!' and waved his hands to invite them over.

'I'll introduce you to a sample, my dear fellow, then you can ask them silly questions yourself. The goat-faced gent is the celebrated Wimbush – him, I know you'll like to meet in person!'

CHAPTER FIVE

G ENTLY TOOK HIS tea in Glove Street, still without having returned to Headquarters. The café was a comfortable little haven, as useful for thinking as for eating. With a paper folded beside him he sat quietly puffing his pipe; a second pot of tea had been served him, and over the radio they were droning the cricket scores.

In all, he'd met four of the Palette Group members, without including their lively chairman. There'd been the youngster, Watts, and the melancholy Wimbush, Seymour, a still-life painter, and Aymas the Ploughman.

He hadn't asked them very much, nor seemed too interested in them; he didn't have the cards in his hand to make a strict interrogation profitable. His principal target had been Aymas, on account of his car, but also because he found him the most original character. And:

'The dead woman, I believe, was a special friend of yours?'

Aymas's ruddy complexion had deepened and his brown eyes became more indignant. He was a little over thirty and of a sturdy, large-framed build. He had a handsome if belligerent face and a romantic shock of thick dark hair.

'But don't you run away with the idea . . . !'

His hard, loud voice carried the stamp of the broad acres. It rose and fell in country cadences, it was sudden and pungent in driving home a point. Gently had asked him where his car had been parked, and Aymas, triumphantly, had told him that it was in Chapel Street.

'Your slops must have sat there looking at it all the evening – if they'd come out in a hurry, it'd have sent them arse over tip!'

All the same, Chapel Street wasn't as remote as was the Haymarket – remembering the footway, in fact, it wasn't remote at all. Of the others only Seymour had had something direct to be asked him: he was one of those who admitted to leaving the cellar before Mrs Johnson.

But it was Mallows himself who had most strongly aroused Gently's interest, sufficiently so to make him want to sit pondering the man. Just now and then one met somebody who stirred one fundamentally – colourful, tantalizing, challenging one to comprehend them. How much lay behind it, that gracefully worn lionskin? What batteries of private emotion lit the façade of public utterance? Mallows had held something back, of this Gently was certain: the academician suspected something which he didn't intend to communicate.

Gently remembered Stephens's hypothesis and his lips parted in a smile. The laugh would be on him if his protégé had made a lucky guess! And perhaps it wasn't so far out either, that diagnosis of blackmail. Mallows would have a lot to lose if his public character were assailed . . .

So absent-minded did Gently become that in going out he forgot his change. A smiling manageress recalled

68

him, and he was not displeased to find that she knew his name.

He made his way across the marketplace, where pigeons were running among the closed-up stalls. The George III, a building coeval with its name, lifted a picturesque face above the brightly coloured tilts. It was tall and narrow and irregularly built, with handsome bow windows on its jutting first storey. The plasterwork had been painted a smooth pale grey, while the windows and elegant iron-work were a complementing shade of green. It stood on a slope and had a towering appearance, and behind it, softly baroque, brooded the majestic bulk of St Peter's church.

In the bar, a few of the stallholders had gathered for a pint and they stared at Gently for a moment as he came up to the counter. The publican, a short man with a finely clipped moustache, wore a tight black waistcoat and was serving in his shirt sleeves.

'Superintendent Gently . . . can I have a word in private?'

The publican winced as though Gently had used a rude word.

'You can see I'm busy, can't you . . . ?'

'I shan't keep you for long.'

'I've heard those tales before! Besides, what else do you want to know?'

But he put his head round the corner, where he shouted something unintelligible, and after a short delay a barmaid appeared. She had a sulky expression and was still smoothing her hair; the publican, after muttering to her, led Gently into the back parlour.

'It plays hell with my reputation, having policemen keep

coming here. You'd think, from the way they do it, that she was knocked off in my cellar!'

'That's something that I want to see, by the way.'

'Why didn't you say so in the first place? We can talk there as well as here.'

The entrance to the cellar was from behind the bar counter, where a divided door gave access to a landing and a steep flight of steps. There was no need to switch on a light since the room below was lit by grating windows; in fact, apart from the staircase, it bore little resemblance to anything cellar-like. The walls were painted in green and cream and the floor was covered with a patterned lino. To the left, with a screen of dusty twigs, was a hearth and fireplace of mottled tiles. An old piano stood over in the corner and on the wall hung a fraying dart board; the floor was furnished with a few marble-top tables, but a number of chairs stood stacked under a window.

'We call it a cellar, but it's just another room. On account of it's awkward to get at, we don't bother with it as a rule. Then a party comes along and wants to have somewhere on their own . . . there's a door into the alley, up that other flight of stairs.'

Gently nodded an absent response and took a few steps about the room. It was a prosaic enough place, that, for painters to hold their meeting in! The green-and-cream decor gave it a frigid, canteen atmosphere, while the carelessly stacked chairs were suggestive of a store. And in the winter, it couldn't have been too well lighted for the viewing of pictures . . .

'Can you hear what's going on when they're having a meeting down here?'

'Not unless the door's open, and we mostly keep it shut. They have so many rows that it disturbs the regular custom – when they want a round of drinks, they come up and knock on the door.'

'But you can hear when they're having a row?'

'Blimey, yes! You can hear them all right.' The publican made an expressive snatching motion with his head. 'But you can't really hear what they're saying, not unless you open the top and listen. It's just a grumbling sound, you get me? Like someone had stirred up a nest of hornets.'

'Was that how it was on Monday night?'

'That's how it was, and a blessed sight worse. You wouldn't believe how they carry on – and they don't drink enough to be anything but sober.'

Gently pulled down a chair and reversed it for himself – not, like Johnson, to bring him luck, but because he preferred to lean on the back. From up the stairs one could hear the faint squeaking of the beer engine, but of the conversation in the bar not even a murmur filtered through.

'You say that it was worse on Monday night?'

'A blessed sight worse, that's what I said.'

The publican also pulled down a chair and, rather awkwardly, emulated Gently.

'Mind you, it started off quietly enough – rather surprised me, it did, at first. As a rule they're pretty well warmed up by eight, which is just about the time when the regulars come in. But last Monday – no; they were like a lot of lambs. They must be mending their ways, I think. Of course, there was a grumble or two now and then, but that wasn't anything to what we're used to.'

'How long did it last?'

'The best part of the evening. There was a darts match in the bar between us and the Bunch of Grapes. Well, they were just coming up to the final throw-off when we heard them letting fly down here in the cellar.'

'What time would that be?'

'Oh, well after nine. We'd had the news on the wireless and then turned it off again. It was just after I'd handed down another tray of drinks – I hadn't hardly latched the door up when they was at it, hammer and tongs.'

'Who was making all the noise?'

'There you are, I wouldn't know. But that bloke they call Aymas was bawling as loud as any. Then Mrs Johnson's voice, I heard that once or twice, and I could hear Mr Mallows as though he were trying to quieten them down.'

'How long did it go on?'

'Up to closing, or thereabouts. Spoiled the darts match it did, they couldn't concentrate through that. We switched the wireless on again, turning it up to kill the noise, but every time the music stopped you could hear them rumbling away.'

Gently rocked his chair thoughtfully – this was a slightly different picture! Mallows had definitely tried to give him an impression of something more pacific. It was lively, he'd admitted, but no more so than other meetings. Nothing out of the way had happened – nothing for Gently to poke his nose into . . .

'Who else was serving in the bar?'

'Dolly, of course. And she's my stepdaughter.'

'She heard what was going on down here?'

'The whole bar heard it – even the deaf ones.'

'I'd like to speak to her, if you'll send her down.'

Dolly was a buxom-figured redhead and she had a pretty, dimpled face. She came down carrying a glass of beer to which no doubt she had just been treated. Gently motioned to the other chair. She sat down, carefully smoothing her skirt.

'You knew Mrs Johnson, did you, Dolly?'

She nodded and sipped at her glass of beer.

'Did you ever have occasion to speak to her?'

'Of course I did. I knew the lot of them.'

'What did you think of her, as a person?'

'I dunno . . . she was queer, in a way. Sometimes she made a lot of fuss of me, other times I was so much dirt.'

'Did you ever meet her outside the pub?'

'Not to speak to nor nothing like that. She'd give me a smile if we met in the street . . . but only when she hadn't got anyone with her.'

'What sort of people did she use to have with her?'

'Oh, that lot mostly, one or another of them. She liked Mr Mallows and the dark boy, Aymas, but they all put it on for her – I'm sure I don't know why.'

'Did you see her with Mr Allstanley?'

'You mean the one who's going bald? I can't say I remember that . . . but then, I didn't see everything, did I? He's one of them who lives out, so you don't see much of him in the pub. But the rest of them often drop in. There's a couple sitting up there now.'

'Was there anyone she was especially . . . fond of?'

Dolly took a thoughtful sip at her beer. 'No . . . not unless it was Stephen Aymas, and she was pally enough with him. I used to think she had a weak spot for money

. . . Mr Mallows, and the one who works at the bank. But Stephen, he only works on a farm, so it couldn't have been money in his case, could it?'

She gazed up at Gently with naive hazel eyes, appealingly unaware of his being anyone out of the ordinary. Her make-up was heavy and clumsily applied; as though it were a ritual which she accepted rather as a duty.

'You didn't chance to meet her husband, I suppose?'

'Oh yes, but I did.' Dolly nodded her head at him assuringly. 'And I'll tell you something about him. He was as jealous as could be. I know for a fact that he used to follow her in the street.'

'You've seen him do that?'

'Yes, I have – and another thing. He once came into the bar when they were having a meeting down here. He had a pint and hung around, trying to see down the hatch, then he asked me right out if Mrs Johnson was at the meeting.'

'How did you know who he was?'

'I told you, I'd met him before. My uncle runs the bar at the golf club and I've been up there to lend a hand. I particularly noticed Mr Johnson – he's got a way with him, you know. Then there's that silly moustache of his, and the way he likes to turn his chair round.'

'This following her in the street! How did you come to notice that?'

'I saw him do it from my window. You can see all the Walk from up in my bedroom, and I just happened to notice her, along with Mr Mallows. Then I saw Mr Johnson. He followed them right up the Walk.'

'When do you say this was?'

'I dunno . . . round about Whitsun.'

'And what about the other?'

'Oh, that was at the meeting last month. He came in here just after it started, and stayed leaning on the bar for a good half-hour. He bought a packet of Players — I remember that especially. It was the last packet, you see, so I had to fetch some more from the store . . .'

'Did you see him again that evening?'

'No. He hasn't been here since.'

When he remembered how nearly he had missed interviewing these people, Gently couldn't help feeling alarmed with himself. It had been touch and go whether he had visited the pub, or had trusted to Hansom's usually efficient researches. Now, it became clear, the Chief Inspector had scamped this angle, for if Dolly's statement had been in his files the Yard would scarcely have been called at all . . .

'Coming to that meeting on Monday!'

He almost made Dolly jump. She had been nursing her beer glass between her knees, causing the contents to rotate. 'I'd like you to tell me everything you can remember about it — even the little things which don't seem to matter.'

'There isn't much to tell, really . . .'

'Never mind. Do your best. Let's have it from the time when the bar opened after tea.'

Dolly nodded and sought inspiration in a sip of beer. 'Well, I'm not in the bar when it opens, not as a rule. For the first hour it's quiet enough, just the men off the market. I did slip in for some fags and stop a moment to have a word with them — they were talking about the new winger, the one the City has bought from Newcastle.

'Then I went back to my bedroom to do a bit of mending – you'd be surprised how I bust the straps off my things! – and out of the window I saw one or two of them arrive – the artist lot, I mean; Mr Mallows and some of the others.

'It's easy to pick them out because they're all carrying pictures, all except Mr Allstanley, who does funny things with wire. And of course, Mr Mallows – he never brings anything. But then, he's rather different from the rest of them, isn't he?'

'Did you see Mrs Johnson?'

'Yes, I'm going to tell you. She always gets off her bus near Lyons. Stephen Aymas went to meet her – he always does that, then sometimes they have a glass in the bar before the meeting.'

'Did they do that on Monday?'

'N-no, I think they went straight down, and it struck me that Mrs Johnson was looking a bit peevish. I watched them across the marketplace, with Stephen chattering away to her; but she hardly said a word to him, and when she did, he seemed put out by it. Something's upset her, I said to myself, and I remember thinking it might have been her husband. Anyway, poor Stephen was getting the edge of it, and that's maybe what made him so angry later.

'Well, I went down into the bar after that – we'd got a darts team coming, and I like to watch a darts match. Now and then there was a knock on the shutter for drinks, but I soon got rid of them and latched up the door again.'

'Did you catch anything of what was going on down here?'

Dolly stared for an instant at her revolving beer. 'They were going on about Mr Wimbush, how he'd used the wrong colours. It's always something like that – they never seem to do anything right! If I painted any pictures I wouldn't show them to that lot . . .'

'Could you hear Mrs Johnson?'

'Oh yes, she was at it. Though I can't remember anything she said, not particular. But I thought the same thing – she was upset about something; she sounded spiteful, you know, as though she wanted to take it out of someone.'

'How many times did they knock for drinks?'

'Two . . . three times, I think it was.'

'And each time you served them you could hear Mrs Johnson?'

'Yes, I told you . . . *and* later on! That was the time when the big row started – half past nine, as near as makes no difference. Me, I was washing up a few of the glasses, and Father was having a Guinness along with Bob Samson. It went off sudden, if you know what I mean. They'd been right quiet just a minute before. Then I heard Stephen Aymas shout something out, angry-like, and before you could say it they were all carrying on.'

'What was it that Aymas shouted?'

'That I can't tell you. I was listening to what father was telling Bob Samson. But later on I heard him bawling that somebody wasn't genuine, and then that they were a liar and hadn't ever told the truth.'

'Who do you think he was referring to?'

'Why, Mrs Johnson, of course. You could hear her shouting back at him, though naturally, not so loud.'

'And did you hear what she said?'

'No, but she sounded more spiteful than ever. You can

lay your hand to your heart that she was the one who set it off. Well, then father switched on the wireless and turned it up as high as it would go – Edmundo Ros, it was, and Victor Silvester after that. The boys went on with their darts match, though it was putting them off a bit . . . they're a useful lot from the Grapes, they went a long way in the Shield . . .'

'Did you hear anything else that was said?'

Dolly shook her head. 'There wasn't much chance. And by the time we'd hung the cloth up, they'd managed to cool themselves off a bit. I went down after their glasses. She'd gone by then, had Mrs Johnson. Those that were left were still muttering to each other, but they dried up when they saw me.

'I asked them what all the fuss was about – like I told you, I know them pretty well; but they shrugged and put me off, said I wouldn't understand it anyway.'

'Was Aymas still in the cellar then?'

'He was leaving just as I was going down.'

'You couldn't give me the time, precisely?'

'Near enough twenty to eleven, I should think.'

Which was almost exactly on cue, if Aymas intended to follow Mrs Johnson – though whether the moment was propitious for offering lifts was a point which a good defence counsel would snatch at. But then, such an offer might not have come into it. The idea of that lift was still hypothetical. And in the meantime a case was slowly tightening around Johnson: they could now show some motive and the appearance of a prior plan.

'In the morning I'd like you to come along and sign a statement.'

'To the police station, you mean?' Dolly looked a little concerned. To have a chat over a beer in the cellar of the George was, apparently, poles apart from the same thing at HQ. Gently grinned at her consternation:

'I give you my promise not to eat you . . .'

Still, she looked as though she thought that she might have been mistaken in him.

The bar, when he returned upstairs, had several more customers in it, and the radio over the cigarette display was playing a Grieg dance. A game of darts had begun, played with private sets of darts: it was plain that the sport was taken seriously by the George III patrons.

The publican touched his arm: 'There's three of the playmates over there . . .'

He motioned with his head towards a table near the door, at which was sitting Phillip Watts in the company of two older men. One of them, from Mallows's description, Gently recognized to be Baxter, and the other, by his smart appearance, he guessed was the bank manager, Farrer. As he studied them Watts looked up, and his eyes encountered Gently's; after a word to his two companions he rose and signalled to the detective.

'Can I offer you a drink, sir . . . ?'

Gently went over to them, shaking his head.

'If I may, sir, I'd like to introduce you . . . I've just been telling them about this afternoon.'

They were, as Gently had supposed, the man from the bank and the poster painter, and it soon transpired that they had a grievance to air. Both their cars had been impounded by the machinations of Stephens; Baxter, who lived far off the bus routes, was particularly biting in his complaints.

79

'I assume that the police *do* have these powers, but all the same, given a modicum of low-grade intelligence . . .'

He was just as Mallows had limned him, with a small, bony head and greying hair; he spoke in a dry and scratchy manner and wore steel-rimmed glasses over deprecating eyes. The pipe that he 'whiffed' at, giving successive little puffs, had a flat round bowl and a spindly stem.

'I suppose it's what you'd call routine, Superintendent . . . ?'

Gently found himself taking a little better to Farrer. He was a good-looking man of not more than forty-five, and though his smile was probably professional, he was at least making use of it.

'You realize that we are obliged to do these things.'

'Of course, Superintendent. But you can't expect us to like them.'

'I could probably arrange some transport for you gentlemen.'

'No, no, don't bother. We'll see it out now.'

He took the opportunity of asking where they had parked their cars on the Monday, though Farrer's, he knew already, had been on the Haymarket. Baxter's, it appeared, had been there also, and after a moment or two's thought Farrer was able to confirm this.

'Do either of you remember where Allstanley put his?'

Farrer pulled himself up short, but Baxter was not so discreet:

'Allstanley comes from Walford – he'd have to come in along St Saviour's.' And he whiffed with his pipe stuck out at a defiant angle.

But when it came to the meeting itself there was a

conspiracy of silence. A curious sort of uncomfortableness seemed to descend on all three of them. It was as though they felt ashamed of the scene which had taken place, and had tacitly agreed to forget all about it.

'I think I ought to tell you that this is important! I am already aware that Aymas quarrelled with the deceased . . .'

Farrer admitted that the two of them had disagreed about a picture, but at the same time insinuated that it could hardly be called a quarrel.

'Yet they were shouting at each other?'

'Aymas's voice is naturally loud.'

'Didn't he call the deceased a liar?'

'He's called me one, too, before now.'

Baxter flatly observed that Aymas was 'naturally choleric', but permitted nothing else to escape past his pipe. As for Watts, he could take a tip from his elders and betters; he simply chimed in assentingly to whatever the others said . . .

The encounter was broken up by the appearance of Stephens, who had apparently come out looking for his errant senior. The young Inspector had a gleam of excitement in his eye, and it was easy to divine that he was fraught with red-hot information.

'Could you come back to Headquarters, sir?'

Gently grunted and rose, nodding his *congé* to the three painters. Since it was too much to expect that Stephens could keep his news till they had returned, Gently took care to steer him the least-frequented way thither.

'What's it about – did you find something in one of the cars?'

'Yes, sir, that is to say, no sir. But I've found something

else! You remember that there was a chummie called Aymas, sir?'

'Aymas!' Gently couldn't keep the interest out of his voice.

'Yes, sir, Aymas. One of those who had a car. Well, he hasn't got it now, sir – he sold it to a firm of breakers. And he sold it on the Tuesday morning, right bang after the murder!'

Gently gave a soft whistle. 'Have you managed to get hold of it?'

'That's the devil of it, sir. The breakers have gone and broken it up. But I've got a man over there, and they're trying to identify the parts, and in the meantime I've taken the liberty of pulling in Aymas for questioning.'

And there was another trifling matter, one which Stephens had almost forgotten. He remembered it only as he was whisking up the steps to HQ:

'Oh, and someone rang you, sir – a person by the name of Butters. He wouldn't state his business to me, and he wants you to ring him back.'

CHAPTER SIX

INSPECTOR HANSOM, THE Lion of Police HQ, had departed to his home shortly after six p.m. He had left a note, however, with the sergeant at the desk, and this was handed to Gently as he passed through with Stephens.

'I thought you'd like to have the low-down on Butters, who rang a couple of times while you were out this afternoon. They're an old county family, used to have the stuff in pots, and they still carry quite a bit of pull about the place. Butters himself is a pal of Sir Daynes Broke. Naturally, we'd be obliged if you soft-pedalled with him.'

Gently grinned to himself as he folded the note away in his wallet. Sir Daynes, the county Chief Constable, was also a pal of his own. It was probably as a result of this common denominator that Butters had insisted on speaking to Gently – rejecting, perhaps ungraciously, the respectful overtures of Hansom. But what had Butters got to do with the demise of Shirley Johnson?

Aymas was sitting alone in the charge room, looking ready to eat a dragon, and he sprang passionately to his feet as Gently peered round the door.

'What the hell do you think all this is about—!' His powerful frame shook with anger and defiance.

Gently shrugged and closed the door again: there was an excellent treatment for angry young men. It consisted of protracting their stay in the charge room, and during a long experience, Gently had rarely known it to fail.

'Good . . . let's go into Hansom's office. It's time we discussed the details together.'

Stephens was reluctant, but deferred to his senior. His hands were soiled with black grease and he had an oil smudge on his nose.

'You drew a blank on the rest of them, did you?'

'Yes, sir, I'm afraid so. Though Baxter's brakes aren't up to standard . . .'

'Where did Allstanley say he parked on that night?'

'Behind the taxi rank, sir, on the island near the market-place.'

'Any verification?'

'Yes, sir, the taxi drivers. He often parks there and it gets in their way.'

So that closed the account of the group members who owned cars, leaving Aymas standing out as the only likely customer. His car had been near the spot if not actually standing on it, and the nearest way to it from the bus stop led directly across the car park.

'It raises one or two problems, though . . .' Gently filled Stephens in on this. 'He could hardly have stabbed her in his car, so why did he sell it to the breakers?'

'He might have had blood on himself, sir, and then traasferred it to the car.'

'It's a possibility, of course – only there wasn't a lot of blood.'

But the point might still be settled by a lucky find at the breaker's yard, though the fact that the parts had been dispersed would weaken the evidence if it came to a case. It would be necessary to prove to the hilt that they had, in fact, come from Aymas's car.

'I'll give you the rest of the dope on Aymas . . .'

Stephens heard him with eyes that glinted; it was plain from the youngster's enthusiasm that he was abandoning his theory of blackmail. Now it was clearly a *crime passionel*, a case of sudden and irresistible impulse. Shirley Johnson had quarrelled with her passionate lover, and with the first weapon to hand he had stabbed her to the heart. Didn't the facts support this thesis? Hadn't they the grounds of an open-and-shut case?

But even as he was building it up, Gently was slowly rejecting the idea. Could it be that Stephens's enthusiasm had sounded a still, small note of warning for him? It was altogether too simple – it didn't harmonize as it should! There were undertones everywhere that produced an overall chord of dissonance. He had got so far into the business that he was beginning to feel it intuitively; it was no use selecting some facts from it to make a pattern that jarred with the remainder.

'It might be best to wait a little . . .'

'You mean, we're not going to charge him tonight?'

Stephens, whose mind had been racing ahead, sounded as disappointed as a child.

'Oh . . . we'll put him through the hoop and see how much we can squeeze out of him. But don't expect him to break down and dump confessions in your lap. For the rest, it depends on tying in his car, and unless you can do that, the Public Prosecutor won't look at it. Now give me the phone – I want to hear what Butters can tell us.'

The number was on the Lordham exchange, and this, at eight p.m., seemed difficult to contact. The Grieg dance which Gently had heard persisted in running through his head, conjuring up, quite irrelevantly, a picture of the rainy Bergen hills. And below them, in the fish market, knives were flashing on the busy slabs, while down the quay, beyond the Tyskebryggen, the *Venus* or the *Leda* waited . . .

'Lordham one-five-eight.'

'This is Superintendent Gently.'

'Ah! I'm very glad to hear it. I've been trying to get you since lunch, sir.'

It was indeed a 'county' voice – a blend of Eton and the hunting field; one imagined that its owner was wearing spurs, or at the least, was flicking a dog whip.

'My name is William Butters and I am acquainted with Sir Daynes Broke. He has always given me to understand that one can talk to you, Superintendent.'

'Is it about the death of Mrs Johnson?'

'Yes, it most certainly is. I have what I feel to be some vital information, and I would like you to call on me without further delay.'

Gently made a face at Stephens. 'Couldn't you tell me over the phone, sir?'

'No, Superintendent, I couldn't. It involves some highly personal explanations.'

In spite of his brusqueness a note of anxiety had crept into Butters's voice – it was as though he wanted to ask a favour, and didn't know quite how to set about it.

'You are busy, sir, I am sure, but I am positive that you

won't be wasting your time . . . this may well affect the whole case. It is essential that you should see me at once.'

'Then if you would care to drive over, sir . . .'

'No, I'm afraid it won't do.'

'Then if you could give me a little idea . . .'

'No, Superintendent. You *must* come here.'

There was obviously no help for it, and Gently hung up with a sigh. Stephens, who had divined the state of affairs, was watching his senior's expression anxiously. Gently gave him a grin:

'You don't have to wait for me, you know. Just carry on with Aymas according to the rules they gave you at Ryton.'

'You mean me . . . I'm to interrogate him?'

'Why not? It's all good practice.'

'But I thought, sir – since a charge is so near—'

Gently chuckled and punched the younger man's shoulder.

The drive out to Lordham took him through familiar country, it being at Wrackstead that he had arrested Lammas, the burnt-yacht murderer. There, and at Lordham Bridge, the moorings were busy with pleasure craft, and Gently needed to drive slowly through the careless crowds of yachtsmen. The address he had been given was The Grange House, Lordham, a premises not to be found without a due amount of inquiry; he was directed down narrow lanes which seemed to have lost their *raison d'être*, and it was by following his instinct that he at last arrived at his destination. It was a moderate-sized property of Regency period, and stood palely among trees on a slope above the River Ent. A portico with an elegant flight of steps graced the front, commanding a panoramic view of the sedgy, twining river. Its decoration, Gently noticed, was not in first-class order, and there were signs of neglect in the rather fine terrace gardens. The garage doors stood apart to reveal a highly polished Rolls, but it was a Rolls of a period which predated the Second World War.

He parked his Riley on the notched tiling in front of the garage, and made his way to the portico, of which the door was also open. Then, quite unconsciously, he threw a glance at the upper windows – to find that a pair of frightened eyes were staring down into his. It was only for a second. In the next, they had disappeared. From such a glimpse he had been unable to register either the sex or age of their owner. An instant later a curtain was pulled, though actually this was quite unnecessary; the room behind it was already darkened by the subdued light of the evening.

'Superintendent Gently, is it?'

He found himself staring blankly at Butters. The man had approached him down the steps and was offering his hand with mechanical politeness.

'I'm glad that you decided to call . . . I'm afraid this interview has been delayed too long. But perhaps if you are a family man, you will appreciate my position . . .'

Gently shook hands and mumbled something in reply – had they been an illusion, those fear-struck eyes? Butters led him into the house and along a wide, deserted hall, ushering him finally into a room which had a faintly mouldy smell. It was large, and period-furnished, but there were pale areas of damp on the wallpaper.

'Can I offer you a drink to begin with . . . ?'

Butters closed the door carefully behind him. He was a man of sixty or over and had a flushed and alcoholic face. His figure had probably once been athletic, but now was thickening and running to fat. He wore a suit of Donegal tweed of which the waistcoat seemed too small for him.

'If you don't mind, I'll have one myself . . . I always talk better with a drink in my hand. But you'd better sit down, Superintendent. This . . . I'm afraid it may take a little time.'

Obediently, Gently took possession of a petit point easy chair, one of a set of half a dozen which stood about the handsome room. Butters seated himself in another and swallowed down some brandy and water. From the slight tremulousness of the glass, Gently suspected that it was not his first.

'Have you ever been to Norway?'

Once again, Gently was staring blankly. It was the merest coincidence, of course, and yet he couldn't help feeling struck by it . . .

'It's a first-rate country for fishing, and I've been up there several times. You take the Bergen Line out of Newcastle – it gets you across in nineteen hours.'

'Is this to do with Mrs Johnson, sir?'

'Yes, and you'll see how in a minute. But let me tell the tale my own way . . . it puts me out when people ask questions.'

Gently held back the ghost of a shrug and fixed his gaze on a French Empire clock. In Butters's manner there was too much of the club bore: one could hear his 'county' tones droning on into the night . . .

'I was there in '53 at a hotel in Stalheim – just Phoebe and myself, the girls were in Switzerland that year. I can recommend the hotel if you're up that way – usual incompetence with meat dishes, but that's the same everywhere. Well, I was fishing one day some miles out of Stalheim, and I dropped into the local *pensjonat* for a spot of *middag*. I was put on a table kept reserved for another Englishman, and this other fellow turned out to be Johnson.

'We fell to talking, of course – a treat to hear your own tongue; I can *snakker* a bit of the native, but only enough to get along with. He told me where he came from and the line of business he was in. Then we got on to the war, and fishing yarns, and places we'd been to . . .'

The upshot of it had been that Butters had taken a liking to Johnson. He had invited him back to his hotel and introduced him to Mrs Butters. Then, their holidays ending together, they had travelled back in company, first by coastal steamer to Bergen and then on the *Venus* home to Newcastle.

'Well, just at that time I was selling my Lynge property, in fact it was already in the hands of an agent. But the local men are much too slow, Superintendent, all they know about selling are these nasty little bungalows . . .'

And so, quite naturally, he'd handed the job to Johnson, and Johnson had come up trumps by the end of a fortnight. He'd produced a retired company director from some-where in Sussex, and what was even better, had got an advanced price from him.

'It was a genuine deal, sir?'

'As genuine as that clock! Nobody can have any complaints about the way he does business. He's keen, sir, and he's got the brains, and he knows where to find the buyers. He's moved off a lot of stuff that had been hanging fire for years.'

'And you recommended him, did you?'

Butters had done, with enthusiasm. He had commended this pearl to his wide acquaintance of 'county' people. As a result Johnson's business had flourished like a bay tree, and he had established a monopoly in the selling of cumbersome properties.

In the meantime, he had cultivated his personal relations with Butters, and had become a familiar visitor at Lordham Grange House. They had fished and played golf and gone sailing in Butters's half-decker, and when Butters went into town, Johnson would take him to lunch at the Bell.

'And that's how it's been going on . . .'

Butters sounded a little petulant; he had already poured himself another brandy and water. Several times, it had seemed to Gently, the man had shied away from something painful, and now he had come to a halt with the matter still unbroached.

'You met Mrs Johnson, did you?'

Butters made some sort of a gesture – half turning, as he did so, so that his eyes avoided Gently's.

'Yes . . . that's just what I want to tell you, but . . . damn it! I don't know where to begin. It'll all come out, I suppose – be plastered across the Sunday papers . . .'

He came to a stop again, and this time Gently forbore to prompt him. It was, after all, a voluntary statement, and Butters had a right to a sympathetic hearing. And, if what Gently guessed was correct, then Butters was showing a good deal of courage . . .

'You understand that we're a county family – not a rich one, I don't say that. But we've got a certain position to keep up ... connections, too. We've got a lot of connections.

'My wife, for example, is a sister of Lady Kempton's – I met her in '23 at the Faverham Hunt Ball. And Cathy, she's married to one of the Pressfords, and Elizabeth's husband is a nephew of Lord Eyleham. Not that that matters – I'm not a snob, either! And though Johnson has no family, I've never held that against him. But the other was a shock, I don't mind telling you, especially when I first saw it staring out of a paper ...'

'The news of his wife's death, sir?' Gently felt that he was losing touch. Butters seemed to have gone off at a tangent from the line he had been about to take.

'Naturally, that too, with the damning implication; but in the first place, to discover that *he'd had a wife at all*!'

It was an astonishing declaration, and for the moment it bewildered Gently. He gazed open-eyed at Butters, who, himself, was now staring indignantly.

'But – in five years – you never knew?'

'I never had a single suspicion! He was on his own when I met him, and as for his flat, I never went there. No, it wasn't until I read the paper – until I saw it in black and white; and even then I couldn't believe it, until I'd had a talk with my daughter.'

'Your daughter! Where does she come into it?'

Butters's stare turned into a furious frown. 'They were engaged – engaged to be married, Superintendent. Or at least, that was the steady impression I received.'

Gently got up and walked over to the window. He felt

unable to cope with this, seated in a chair. Johnson . . . engaged to one of Butters's daughters! To the daughter of the man who had been the making of his business . . .

'And this engagement had been announced?'

'Obviously not, though we were expecting it. All the time I'd been hinting at it, trying to bring him up to scratch. His excuse was that he was looking for just the right sort of property for them; when he found it, there was going to be a regular announcement.'

'How long had it gone on?'

'Oh, he met her right at the start. But in those days she was still at Girton – what a waste of money that was! Then, soon after she finished there, they took to going about together – he wasn't the match I would have picked for her, but she was the youngest, and nothing went with her. They've been thick for a couple of years.'

'And she – she knew about his wife?'

'I've got to admit it. She knew about everything. She was his mistress all the while, and she says she's going to have his baby.'

Over these last few words Butters seemed to have difficulty, and there was no reason to doubt the genuineness of his emotion. One could easily imagine the horror with which he had glimpsed those banner headlines, and then had heard, from his daughter's mouth, that they were trapped in the ghastly business . . .

'You did well, sir, to speak up.'

What was the use of a reprimand? Could he be blamed for taking four days to screw his courage to the sticking point?

'As you said on the phone, this is vital information . . . I think it may enable us to tie up the case.'

Butters swallowed a gulping draught of his brandy and water, and Gently was glad that the deepening twilight made the room behind him shadowy. Below him, down the romantic but deteriorating terrace gardens, a smoke mist was rising mysteriously from the still, silica-like river.

'You don't have to tell me that I should have spoken before . . . in your place, Superintendent . . . but I won't stoop to excuses. I knew on the spot that Johnson had murdered his wife, and I knew that it was my business to put a rope round his neck.

'But God, when it's a question of your own flesh and blood! And, to a certain extent, I had other people to think of . . . And again, it looked at first as though they wouldn't need my help – up till yesterday, even, I thought they were going to arrest him.

'Then that picture business happened and the police seemed to be confused. All night I was pacing that hall . . . I reached for the phone a dozen times.

'I thought of getting on to Sir Daynes, in spite of the fact that it wasn't his business. And I knew the Inspector on the case, but in the past . . . I won't go into that! Then in the morning I saw you had been called, which wouldn't have happened unless they'd been stuck . . . and then I knew I daren't wait any longer. My only consolation was that you were the man . . .'

Gently silently sighed to himself – so near, it had been, to his *not* being the man! He wondered how Butters would have got on with Stephens, who would almost certainly have read him a lecture.

Wouldn't that reference to the county Chief Constable have got Stephens's back up, straight away?

'You might have confided in Sir Daynes, sir . . .' He heard the clink of glass and decanter.

'Yes . . . I think I might have done that. Failing you, I think I might have done it. But not that other fellow, Hansom . . . as I say, a motoring offence . . . Yet, since Tuesday, I've been in hell . . . God, I couldn't help feeling responsible!

'If I'd been a proper parent I would never have let it go on. I had a suspicion, once or twice, that things weren't as innocent as they seemed. But in these days everything is different . . . I didn't want to look a fool . . . and I trusted him, you know. I was sure he wouldn't let me down.

'That's the most damnable thing about it. I liked the fellow, and encouraged him! And to think, that by doing that, I was driving him to desperation . . .

'If I'd found out about his wife he would have lost Anne and most of the business . . . it only wanted her to become pregnant . . . you see how inevitable it was? There was no other way out, he was forced to do something. His wife was a wrong 'un, it appears, and she wouldn't give him a divorce . . .'

Gently turned from the window and came slowly back into the room. Butters was leaning over his knees, his umpteenth brandy shaking in his hand. He wasn't cut for a tragic figure and his posture looked at first sight comic; yet this very misfortune, paradoxically, had the effect of emphasizing his pathos. And behind him, the damp-stained wallpaper took on the office of a symbol . . .

'You have questioned your daughter, I take it?' He remembered the frightened eyes which had watched him.

'She's . . . I've kept her in the house since Tuesday; as a prisoner, if you like . . .'

'What was she doing on the Monday evening?'

Butters shuddered. 'If you don't mind, Superintendent . . .'

'Very well . . . fetch her down, then. I shall have to see her myself.'

While Butters was absent from the room, Gently made a leisurely and appraising tour of it. In the grey and absorbing twilight he was probably seeing it at its best. Unlike a period piece restored, it lacked a logical unity of style; it had gathered one or two Victorian pieces, and even some items of a later date.

The pictures, however, apart from two portraits, were all landscapes representing the local school. Gently identified a Stark and a pair of Ladbrookes, and a cottage scene which was probably by Vincent. But of their master, Crome, he could discover no trace – but then, he was probably a death duty too late.

His prowling was interrupted by the switching on of the light, and he turned to find Butters pushing his daughter into the room. He had been holding her by the arm, which he now released, and he was prompt in closing and bolting the door.

'I'd prefer to be present, if I may, Superintendent.'

Gently nodded, and motioned Anne Butters to a chair. Even now she hadn't quite lost that look of terror, though added to it, Gently saw, was a seasoning of defiance.

She was a shapely, slender girl with a pale-complexioned oval face, and golden-brown hair which she wore long and slinky. She had pale green eyes under fine, symmetrical brows; they gave a touch of distinction to a face which was inclined to be plain.

'This is a serious business, I'm afraid, Miss Butters.'

She was wearing a plain green dress, the skirt of which was gracefully flared. As he spoke to her, he noticed that she tightened her lips together; there were angry marks on her arm where it had been held by her father.

'Tomorrow, I shall want you to give me a regular statement at the police station. Just now, I would like you to answer a few questions I shall put to you.'

'It wasn't Derek who killed her!' She hissed the words out rather than spoke them, her green eyes sparking at him from lids which jumped suddenly open.

'I didn't say it was. Now, if you'll be good enough to listen—'

'He was with me the whole evening – we were in bed. So there!'

With a quick, hysterical movement she jerked back the flared skirt, revealing a pair of neat legs and a froth of black lace. Her father started forward, but she immediately dropped the skirt again. Then she turned to him like a child, making a sneering, triumphant face.

'Do you want me to tell you some more? I'm sure you'd love to have it in detail! My father would, in any case – he adores a bit of smut! We began at half past seven—'

'Anne – that's quite enough of that!'

'—at half past seven, he undressed me—'

'For heaven's sake, pull yourself together!'

Once more Butters started towards her, though what he could have done was problematical; before he could get to her, however, she had burst into a storm of tears.

'He didn't do it, I tell you, oh, Derek didn't do it! You'll never understand, but he didn't – he didn't do it!'

Somebody banged on the door and then fruitlessly rattled the handle. Butters fumbled it open and disappeared into the hall. A low colloquy could be heard, its substance drowned by Anne's sobbing, but its rise and fall suggested that Butters was trying to reassure his wife.

In the background, with senseless monotony, an electric pump was thumping away.

'I've got to apologize . . . it's very difficult . . .'

Butters returned, and went at once to the decanter. His eyes were watering as though from a chill, and besides being flushed, his face was puffy and ugly. It was not unlikely that he was already drunk, but he carried himself steadily and it was difficult to tell.

'My dear, for your own sake . . .'

He bent over his daughter. She had overcome her sobbing and was now using her handkerchief.

'She's like her mother, you know . . . they're both highly strung. It runs in the family. Phoebe is allied to the Fitz-Morrises . . .'

Gently began again, trying to take it very easily. Anne Butters, as though ashamed of herself, listened meekly to his questions. Yes, she had 'always' known that Derek Johnson was married. Yes, she had entered the association with eyes wide open. She had been his mistress for two years, and she really was pregnant. They had always 'taken precautions', but once or twice they had been rather rash.

'Did you used to go to his flat?'

She tossed her locks at him disdainfully. 'We weren't quite such congenital idiots as to walk in on his wife.'

'Where did he used to take you then?'

'Oh, it was anywhere at first. The yacht, the car, or a

nice quiet wood – to begin with, we weren't much worried by discomforts.'

'But after that?'

'We sometimes went to his office, only that was too risky to make into a regular thing. So Derek bought a furnished cottage – I suppose I can tell you about it now; it's at the end of a lane, about a mile from Nearstead.'

'Did you ever meet his wife?'

'I looked her over once or twice. She was a bitch, as you probably know, and it didn't surprise me that she was murdered.'

'What did Derek say about her?'

'He said she was queer, and that she liked other women.'

'Didn't he ever talk about a divorce?'

'Yes. He said he'd divorce her when he got the evidence.'

She became bolder as the questioning proceeded, trying to compensate perhaps for her tears; her eyes she kept staring steadily into Gently's, almost challenging him to do his worst with her. Butters, his glass never out of his hand, sat frowningly watching her from a seat near the door.

'Where did you meet him on the Monday night?'

'In the usual place – at the top of the lane.'

'And then he drove you straight to the cottage?'

'Yes. We arrived there before half past seven.'

'And what time did you leave again?'

'At eleven o'clock, or a few minutes after.'

Gently hunched his shoulders wearily. 'Perhaps you would like to reconsider those estimates?'

For an instant it seemed that she didn't understand him, her eyes slowly widening in interrogation. Butters, however, understood very well, and he made a helpless gesture with his hand.

'It's no use, Anne . . . he knows you're lying.'

'Keep out of this, you . . . !'

'My dear, it's no use. I . . . we all know what time you came in.'

'Shut up – do you hear?'

'It was at five past ten . . .'

They were trembling on the brink of another hysterical outburst. Her slim body was twitching and shuddering with emotion. But then, after a fit of glaring, she tossed her head away from her father, and contented herself with hitching her skirt a couple of inches above her knees. Butters swigged down some brandy and affected not to see it.

'Very well, then – I told a lie! But don't forget that I'm a harlot. You're lucky to get a ha'porth of truth from a person such as I am.'

'Perhaps I should tell you something, Miss Butters.'

'Why not? It's a favourite game of my father's.'

'Derek Johnson's account of that evening doesn't square with what you have told me.'

She burst into a mocking peal of laughter. 'And did you expect him to tell you the truth? Did you expect he was going to tell you that he was shacked up with Butters's daughter? He spun you a yarn, of course he did. He never dreamed that my father would betray him. He used to be in the RAF, where you could depend on your friends to stand by you!'

'But naturally, we checked his account.'

'There you are then – you knew it was a lie.'

'But that is just what we don't know, Miss Butters. His account is apparently confirmed by our checking. He made a round of some of the pubs, and a number of people can remember having seen him. So I'm afraid I must put this question to you: how did *you* spend that evening, Miss Butters?'

Her pallid cheeks grew paler still, and her eyes, by contrast, appeared to grow larger. Butters had gone off in a coughing fit – he had spilled some brandy on the carpet.

'I was home by five past ten – I didn't go out again after that!'

Gently turned to the spluttering Butters:

'It's true . . . she had a bath and went to bed.'

'But what were you doing during the evening?'

'It's as I said – I was out with Derek!'

'But nobody has mentioned seeing you with him.'

'He – he brought me the drinks out to the car.'

Was she still lying, or was it the truth? Gently stared long at those flaming green eyes. As though it were an indicator of her good faith, she was quietly pushing her skirt back into place.

'I *was* with him, all the evening, though I admit that we were going round the pubs. I only said that about the cottage because I thought you were more likely to believe it. But I was with him from a quarter past seven, and we were together until he dropped me at ten – I never stayed out later than that. It would have started my father prying.'

'When had you told him that you were pregnant?'

'Oh, weeks ago – as soon as I was certain.'

'What did you intend to do about that?'

'Derek was trying to find a good abortionist.'

'Did he speak of his wife on Monday?'

She pouted. 'You wouldn't believe he didn't! Well, he said he was certain that she was carrying on with an artist, but that she was being very clever, and that he was thinking of hiring a detective.'

'Did he say who it was he suspected?'

'No. She was playing about with several of them. But that was what he intended to do, and not to stick a paper knife in her back!'

Gently let it go at that, sensing further emotional fireworks – in the morning he would have another chance to see what he could chivvy out of her. Butters, in great relief, hustled his daughter out of the room; Gently thoughtfully lit his pipe and blew some smoke at the collecting mosquitoes.

A most illuminating hour! He glanced at the fallen level in the decanter. Down by the river some points of light showed where a yacht or two had made their moorings. In spite of his pipe he could smell the mustiness which persisted in the room, and he noticed a patch of mould that was growing on the paper beneath the window.

'Do have a drink, Superintendent . . .'

Now, it was certain that Butters was drunk. He had to be careful where he put his feet, and his watering eyes had a bemused expression.

CHAPTER SEVEN

A T LORDHAM VILLAGE, where he stopped to phone, Gently experienced an even longer delay with the exchange. The country operator answered him with a surly briefness, as though this was really laying it on too thick.

'Can you bring Inspector Stephens to the phone . . . ?'

His wristwatch was pointing to a minute to ten. As he could hear Stephens picking up the phone to answer him, the hour struck fussily on the church clock outside.

'How is the session with Aymas going?'

In reality he could tell this from the sound of Stephens's voice.

'I'm afraid he's been terribly stubborn up till now, sir . . . you were quite right about him not breaking down and confessing.'

'What excuse does he give for sending his car to the breakers?'

'He persists in maintaining that that was all it was fit for. He says that he only kept it till Tuesday on account of Monday night's meeting, and that he's negotiating for a better one, and hopes to buy it tomorrow.'

'Have you checked on that?'

'Yes, sir. With the vendor. He agrees that Aymas spoke to him about it over a fortnight ago.'

Gently clicked his tongue consolingly. 'I wouldn't worry too much about it! Just smooth Aymas down a bit and find him some transport. Then I want you to go out and to pull in Johnson for questioning . . . take another man with you. I want to talk to Johnson tonight.'

He hung up before Stephens could ask him for an explanation. He felt no particular exhilaration at being in possession of the conclusive facts. They had come to him by pure good fortune and through no exertion of his own, unless his luck could be counted, the luck that dogged a good detective. And that luck would have belonged to Hansom if Gently had not been called to the case.

Or would it? He stood brooding, his hand on the Riley's door, partly conscious of the buzz from the pub across the way. If Gently hadn't arrived, wouldn't Butters have continued to procrastinate, probably drowning his courage, at last, in the bottom of the decanter? That was at least on the cards. Butters had much to gain from silence. And nobody had actually seen Johnson thrust that knife into his wife. There was a damning case, certainly, one which would convince any jury, but juries had made mistakes before, and there was a sop left for the conscience . . .

Gently pulled the door open with a grunt of annoyance. He too was finding a degree of temptation in this viewpoint! But the facts were the facts, and they hung together in a perfect symmetry; unless the circumstantial were accepted, there were cases one would never close.

Before he started back he scraped out his pipe and relit it. The evening was continuing fine and the sky was dusted over with stars. As he drove he could see before him the soft umbrella of the city's lights, at first no more than a shallow mushroom, then spreading out to suffuse the horizon.

Then, with the first of the street lights, the luminosity abruptly ended: at precisely that point the country ended and the town began its authority.

He hadn't hurried on the way back, wanting to give Stephens time to act, and now, threading through the haphazard streets, he slowed the Riley to a crawl. He was in an indecisive mood. He would have liked time to think, and yet wanted to be doing. He was conscious of a growing irritation without being able to assign a single reason for it. Was he even sorry, perhaps, that the case was caving in so suddenly – sorry, and just a little bit suspicious? There was something about it which had got under his skin!

When he arrived at HQ he went through to the canteen, and bought himself there a plate of sandwiches and some coffee. While the former were being cut he strolled across to the window, and drawing aside a rep curtain, stared out at the car park. It was true that there wasn't a lot of light in the park. The distant lamps of St Saviour's showed precious little here. A better source of illumination was the wall lamp in the footway, but even by this the terrace wall was merely a dim shadow. And it was fifteen minutes to eleven . . . and four days later.

'Miss . . . were you serving here on Monday night?'

The counter assistant was a homely woman with hair which she had dyed to a bluish tint.

'Yes . . . I'm regular on nights this week. But I didn't hear anything – didn't want to, either! And I'm keeping those windows bolted shut, from now on . . .'

He nodded sympathetically, glancing round the empty canteen.

He found Stephens waiting for him in Hansom's office. The younger man had got his pipe on and was puffing away at it earnestly.

'I grabbed him at the first try! Have you got something fresh on him? He was just putting his car away, and made a devil of a stink . . .'

Gently himself was feeling weary and droop-eyed, but Stephens looked as fresh as he had done that morning. He walked up and down while describing his interrogation of Aymas, drawing briskly on the pipe as he paused between sentences.

'So you think, sir, that after all . . . ?'

He was revelling in the case – far from being discouraged, he was eager to grapple with the newest angle. Gently, busy with his sandwiches, gave his Lordham findings disconnectedly. More than ever he was wondering if he ought not to have slept on them.

'So you guessed it all along, sir!' Nothing, apparently, escaped Stephens. Now he remembered Gently's quip when they were discussing Johnson at tea.

'You were on to it from the start – you could begin to see the *pattern*.'

'Don't talk a lot of poppycock! There wasn't any pattern to see.'

Stephens was unconvinced, however, and puffed away at a furious rate. Gently slyly watched the young man while polishing off the rest of the sandwiches. He was so intent to learn! Yet his very keenness got in the way. He was for ever looking for a formula where no formula could exist. But, further back than he could remember, hadn't it been the same way with Gently? Hadn't he also admired his seniors and striven to find their recipe for success?

'Go and find us a stenographer . . . we may be in for an all-night session.'

He suddenly remembered Herbie the Fence, and was surprised that that had been only yesterday.

If Johnson had made a fuss when Stephens had pulled him in, he had succeeded in calming himself during his wait to see Gently. When a detective ushered him in he was smoking a cigarette and, without being invited, he spun a chair and threw himself down in it. Then he stuck a hand in his pocket with an air of being bored, and jingled his change while hissing smoke through his teeth.

Stephens now occupied a chair beside Gently, and their shorthand constable was stationed at the end of the desk. At the other end was standing a freshly ordered jug of coffee, adding its own fragrant ingredient to the atmosphere of tobacco smoke. In front of Gently, as usual, was a pad for him to scribble patterns on.

'There are some further questions which I have to put to you, Mr Johnson.'

He was drawing a number of parallel lines, greatly to the interest of the observant Stephens.

'But first, I'm going to give you a chance to amend your former statement to us. I should tell you that it doesn't agree with our latest information.'

Johnson continued to smoke noisily for a moment or two, though he had ceased to jingle the change in his pocket. He was gazing with apparent interest at the toes of his shoes, his legs being folded and stuck out in front of him.

'So that's the way of it, is it, cocker?' He ventured a glance at the wooden-faced Gently. 'I thought an old fox like you would sniff the hen roost before long – you wouldn't have snaffled me at this time of night for nothing.'

'Have you anything to tell me?'

'Not until I see the cards, pardner.'

'My information relates to the Butters family.'

'What do you advise? Shall I scream for a lawyer?'

There was no sign of panic about the wavy-haired ex-pilot. One would almost have said that he had taken advice already. A bulky, powerful figure in a lightweight tweed jacket, he sat casually at ease and blew his smoke at varying angles.

'You don't seem to be aware of the gravity of your situation.'

'I should be, old sport. It's my neck that we're discussing.'

'And you don't want to modify your former statement?'

'No reason to do that – it's substantially correct.'

'Didn't you say that you'd never been unfaithful to your wife?'

Another pause followed, during which Stephens jiffled restlessly. Gently imagined that this was not the way in which his protégé had handled Aymas. For at least a minute Johnson was silent, his attention still fixed on the upturned shoes; then he appeared to think better of it, and stubbed his cigarette in Hansom's ashtray.

'The Butters are friends of mine – at least, I used to think so. If you like, you can add that on the bottom of the statement.'

'They were friends and no more?'

'Butters put business in my way.'

'Why didn't you tell him that you were married?'

'It was something that I preferred to forget.'

'And you did forget it, didn't you?' Gently hatched his lines with swift strokes. 'I understand that Anne Butters is going to have a baby.'

'Am I supposed to know that?'

'I'm giving you every chance to tell me.'

'That's jolly decent of you, considering the circumstances.'

He lit another cigarette, flicking the match into the ashtray, and now it was the matchbox which he elected to study. There was no doubt about it – he was a cool customer to interrogate. Was he still picturing himself as a hero before the Gestapo?

'What prisoner-of-war camp were you in?'

'I was in Stalag three-two.'

'Did you ever try to escape?'

'Twice. Once I nearly got to Denmark.'

'Were you treated very harshly?'

'Cocker, don't make me laugh. I was grilled for twenty days and twice they took me out to shoot me. They wanted to know who planned the break, and if they're alive, they're still ruddy well wanting. So you can make up your mind to one thing.' He sent smoke hissing in all directions.

Gently nodded. 'Then there's no more to it. I won't waste my time in the steps of the Gestapo. To *them* you were a Royal Air Force officer, but to me you are just another criminal.'

It hit the spot; Johnson's colour rose. He sucked in an enormous lungful of smoke.

'Don't take that line with me, old sport—!'

'I'm not taking any line – but I'll tell you the truth.'

Now it was Gently who had the pause to play with, and he occupied it in stroking off an entirely fresh pattern. Both Stephens and Johnson were now following the swept motions, only the shorthand man seeming proof against their fascination.

'On the Monday night you had come to a crisis – not an emotional crisis, but a business one. I don't think you gave a damn about losing Anne Butters. An ex-bomber pilot in an MG could soon pick up something else.

'But you cared a great deal about your lucrative business, and you knew that it would take a knock if ever Butters turned against you. He knew the right people. He had sent you the best part of your clients. And he could, just as easily, put the evil eye on you.

'So that was the thing which you had to preserve: the goodwill of William Butters, and your steady flow of clients. And the only way to do that was to marry his daughter, to make good the role you played of being an honourable man. Until Anne became pregnant the matter had no great urgency. You could fob off the pair of them with suitable excuses. You could tell *him* that you were waiting to buy a property that suited you, and *her* that you were still seeking the grounds for a divorce.

'But once she became pregnant the situation began to run away with you, and you had to cast about to find a way out of the tangle. What was more, you needed a way which wouldn't alienate Butters — he was due for a shock, of course; but it was essential not to make him an enemy.

'No doubt you reviewed the possibilities, of which there were three in number. The first of them, abortion, was the one which you mentioned to Anne. But abortion had grave objections, besides being dangerous in itself: how could you keep the family from knowing, and what effect would it have on Anne? Then there was the possibility of blackmail, which I dare say crossed your mind. So, on the whole, you didn't favour abortion, except as another excuse to amuse Anne.

'So you were brought to the second alternative, that of the divorce of which you had talked for so long. As to grounds, you probably had plenty, and without recourse to private detectives. But here again the objections were insuperable. You had to proclaim yourself perjured to Butters. Anne you were sure of if the divorce went through, but she was no use to you unless with her father's blessing. Also, wasn't there a chance that he might have spiked that divorce for you? With divorce, the odds were that you would have come off with nothing.'

Gently discontinued his doodling to look hard at the estate agent, whose frowning grey eyes had never left the busy pencil. Stephens, his pipe between his teeth, was sitting as stiff as a cleaning rod. Tobacco smoke drifted lazily towards the harsh strip lighting.

'Which left you with the third possibility: murder.'

Gently tore off the sheet and crumpled it into the office waste basket.

'It meant risking everything, but you were a man used to risks – and the reward for it was everything that you had hoped to gain. Oh, I realize that Butters was going to have his suspicions, and that his suspicions would be near certainties when he learnt of Anne's condition. But you banked on the initial shock of the affair to shut his mouth, and afterwards – by then, he was halfway to being an accomplice.

'You would have had him where you wanted him! He wouldn't dare, then, to discountenance you. He would feel that he shared the guilt, or perhaps persuade himself that there was none. And Anne's baby would be the clincher: it would ensure that the marriage went through – with a little delay, of course, a little subterfuge – just enough to sink Butters some further!

'I don't know at what stage you made up your mind, but the Palette Group was always waiting to provide you with scapegoats. Your wife went about with them, ate with them, perhaps slept with them – you had plenty of time to find out about that. So, naturally, you arranged to take advantage of the Palette Group. You would murder your wife on their doorstep, so to speak. You checked what her movements were when she attended one of their meetings, and you decided that the car park would best suit your plan.

'Next you needed an alibi, or at least a story that would check – you were clever enough to risk not producing a perfect alibi. Thus instead of going to Nearstead you went off on a round of the pubs, keeping Anne concealed in your car in case the police heard tell of her later. Then, after

112

dropping her at ten, you drove quickly back to town; you parked your car, I think, in Chapel Street, to avoid having it seen in the park.

'You took your stand by the City Hall, probably at the St Saviour's end, and when your wife came by you accosted her, telling her that you were just driving back to the flat. She accepted a lift and went with you. You led her past the bus stop and into the park. As you approached the terrace wall you contrived to drop behind her, and strangling her scream with your arm, you drove the knife into her back.

'She died instantaneously and without much bleeding. You threw her down behind the dustbins, tossing her handbag after her. Then you walked back to your car by the footway at the end here, and drove home, probably arriving at the time given in your statement.

'You made only one mistake – you thought that Butters hadn't got any guts.

'But, in spite of his bottle of brandy, he has just committed you to the hangman!'

The silence that marked the end of his accusation was made the more telling by the murmurs from without – the voice and footfall in the building, the drone of a car from Chapel Street below. Johnson kept frowning at the moving pencil, his childlike lips hung slightly open. He seemed unconscious of the scene about him, unconscious, even, of Gently's presence.

Was he trying, with desperate concentration, to find a plausible way out of this trap?

'Poor Shirley!' – the words came huskily. 'She was a bitch, but Christ . . . she was human.'

113

Gently sighed to himself and reached out for the jug of coffee. He was never at his best, making speeches of that sort. They required an indignation, a degree of faith in moral judgements: to himself, at all events, they never quite rang true. He poured a cup of coffee and tossed it off in three quick gulps. Stephens cast an eye at the cup, then he folded his arms and leaned them on the desk.

'That's the way it was done, of course . . .'

'I'm glad to find you agreeing with me.'

'Hell, but it wasn't me!'

Gently preserved an unimpressed silence.

'Look, cocker . . .' Johnson was stumbling, making beating motions with his hand. 'You've had your fun . . . all right – I don't mind! . . . But it won't stand up . . . I never dreamed of killing Shirley!'

'I think I should warn you, Mr Johnson.'

'I know all about that – and I don't care a damn! You can take it down if you want to, you can print it off on toilet paper. But I'm warning you, cocker, your imagination's running away with you . . . you've cooked up a case, and it won't convince a flea!'

Gently grunted indifferently and felt for his pipe and pouch. He had issued Johnson a warning, and now the ball lay with him. Rather sooner than he had intended he had made this concession, though in view of the facts it probably mattered very little. He filled his pipe with scrupulous care, pressed it down and struck a match.

'You've figured out the way of it – good! I was wondering about that. I couldn't think how he'd got her there, unless . . . it doesn't matter! But you're tackling the wrong kiddie . . . I don't care what you've found out . . .

114

'I've had to listen to your version – now just you listen to mine!'

He could hardly find the words, so fast did he want to bring them out; the stenographer's pencil sounded like a mouse as it nibbled at the paper. Johnson's legs weren't folded now. He was leaning forward towards the desk. His frowning brow was creased with ridges and his eyes were staring and protruded.

'I'm glad that Butters had the sense to speak up . . . it was me who hadn't got the guts! I knew you'd hold it over my head – I could see that coming from the start. But I'm glad, you understand? Because I'm fond of old man Butters! You can say what you like about his bottles of brandy – he's a decent old stick, and I'm here to say so.

'And I like his wife . . . I like his family . . . and Anne, she isn't just the floozie you seem to think her!

'She's my wife, you understand? Not the way that Shirley was! But she's my wife all the same, in spite of not having been to church. She loves me and I love her . . . it's been like that ever since we met . . .

'And I didn't give a damn about the blasted business. I'd have thrown it all up for a chance to marry Anne . . .'

Stephens, who had begun to sneer, was now gazing at Johnson in perplexity; he also glanced in Gently's direction, trying to glean a cue from his senior. This wasn't at all what he had expected to hear from a man with a murder tied on him! Johnson was blurring an open and shut case, he was upsetting its nice, clean lines . . .

'Something else . . . I didn't have anything on Shirley. She was too darned clever to give me a chance! You'll

115

never understand, because you never met her alive . . . as for offering her a lift . . . it's funny, don't you see?

'She was a sadist – she liked to see other people squirm. She got a kick out of sticking to me, though we couldn't stand each other. But if you think for a minute . . . I'm not going to blame her! . . . Only that's the way she was, and you've got to accept the facts.

'And I did try for a divorce, whether it would have mucked me up or not – it wouldn't have done, either. Butters wouldn't have let me down! Just ask my solicitor . . . I've talked it over with him. But I didn't want a detective, I tried to do the job myself, and the long and the short of it was that I never caught her at anything . . .

'Then that alibi – that's rich! My God, I could have done better than that. But the whole idea is cockeyed – we always hit the pubs on a Monday. On Sundays we used to visit the cottage, and you don't need me to tell you . . . so on Mondays we toured the pubs – having a rest, if you want it in words!

'And the abortion, too – did you ever try to fix one? You'd be surprised just how easy it isn't! You've only got to hint at abortion to a medico, and the next minute he's slinging you out on your ear. Then, after a couple of clangers like that . . .

'In any case, I was dead against the idea . . . when I'd talked Anne round a bit, I was going to have it out with Butters. You think you know Butters, but you don't, and that's a fact. When he'd realized how it was with Shirley . . . hell, there's nobody who's quite an angel!'

He was brought up at last by sheer lack of breath and sat for some moments panting, a blond lock fallen across his forehead. The stenographer dropped his pencil on the desk and, in massaging his fingers, produced an unusual cracking sound. Then he selected another pencil from a supply in his breast pocket.

'I know how it looks to you and I don't blame you for a moment . . . but you can't know, you're only guessing about things that really matter.

'What do you know about me, for instance? You only met me seven hours ago! You look at my car, at this moustache . . . and then you tack a label on me.

'It says: "Flying Officer Kite" – all right, so I deserve it! But do you know how people came to be Flying Officer Kites? They were scared into being them – scared silly by what they were doing! They were driven into behaving like clots by sheer terror. Because there aren't any heroes in the whole state of nature . . . only cowards, who one day get shoved into the breach . . .

'But underneath that, what do you know about me? You must be able to see how crazy it all is. By guessing and a few facts you've made me out to be inhuman – an egoistic monster, a psychopath at the very least! And I'm not – I'm not like that. It's too utterly bloody ridiculous. Get on to my friends – I've got plenty of them! The worst they can call me is a line-shooting bastard . . . I'm human, I tell you, I'm not a bloody monster . . .'

He flung the hair out of his eyes and dragged his chair closer to the desk; with his hands gripping the edge of it, he was only a couple of feet from Gently.

'Listen to what I tell you, cocker . . . I want to see that swine collared too! Not out of revenge, or anything like that, but because he ought to be put inside. Shirley . . . you know how I felt about her. She wasn't any credit to the human race. But damn it, she had a right to live, and only a madman would take it away from her . . .

'But now you're playing the madman's game, because it was someone who knew about me and Anne. He gambled that you'd pin it on me for certain, as soon as the rest of the tale came out. So for Christ's sake try to see this straight – I wouldn't have laid my little finger on Shirley!

'On Monday night I did just what I told you. I was never near here, and I didn't kill my wife . . .'

Gently had never stopped puffing at his pipe, but now he put an entirely gratuitous match to it. Having done that, he broke the match in two pieces and arranged them fastidiously in the ashtray.

Always, with Johnson, it was the selfsame question – was he being honest, or was he being clever? Before, they had given him the benefit of the doubt, and even now he was keeping his foot in the door. He had no defence against the charge, and yet . . . what was the answer going to be?

'Take Mr Johnson back to the charge room, will you?' He swung on Hansom's revolving chair, so that his back was towards them. From the reluctant way in which Stephens got to his feet, Gently knew that the Inspector was critical of the order.

'You're holding me . . . is that it?'

'I may want to ask some more questions.'

'And meanwhile I'm in custody?'

'You are assisting the police . . .'

They took him out while Gently was still savouring the irony of the phrase.

Stephens came back quickly, his face wearing a worried look.

'Super, I don't know . . .'

'Sit down and light your pipe.'

'Yes, sir. But my impression—'

'Take a seat! I'm trying to think.'

Stephens did as Gently bid him with the best grace possible, but his pipe, that pride and joy, seemed unable to absorb him. Gently continued to face the wall, his cogitations marked by smoke rings; Stephens was not the first person to have noticed that the Super's back was like an iron curtain.

'So you'd slap him inside, and no more nonsense?'

Ten minutes had passed in the silent smoke rings.

'Under the circumstances, sir—'

'I've got no option. But suppose I was damn fool enough to make myself the option?'

Stephens was thoroughly unhappy and didn't know what to say. He had never before come across Gently in this awkward, angular mood.

'I must admit, sir . . . to my way of thinking . . .'

'Just tell me straight out, Stephens.'

'Very well, sir. I wouldn't think twice about it. He's our chummie, and we'd get a conviction.'

'Hmm.' Some more smoke rings rose towards the ceiling, and again the office was broodingly silent. Then suddenly Gently swivelled round in the chair, the ghost of a grin spreading over his face.

'I always like to ask someone's advice when I'm in danger of making a fool of myself! You are perfectly right about Johnson, of course. No jury would give him twenty minutes.'

119

'Then we'll go ahead and charge him, sir?'

'No, just get him to amend his statement.'

'But I don't understand—!'

Gently's grin grew broader. 'That's exactly what Johnson was trying to tell us . . .'

Once more he was rebelling against the accepted order, and once more he was positive that he was doing the right thing. He wished that he could have explained himself to Stephens, but how could one explain an unreasoning intuition? It was a faculty which had to grow, there was no passing it on.

As it was, he simply patted Stephens on the arm.

'Don't look so upset! I'm going to put a tail on him. If he tries to do a bunk we'll pull him in fast enough. In the meantime, I don't want to tie my hands with Johnson.'

'But if ever there was a case where circumstantial evidence . . .'

'I know. But Johnson made one very good point. We haven't been here long and we don't really know the people . . . why he said it doesn't matter. We can afford to take our time.'

In the end he had Stephens partly propitiated; the young detective, though apprehensive, was eager to follow where Gently led. Johnson's statement was revised, typed out and signed. Nobody had very much to say apart from the bare requirements of the transaction.

'But I can take it that I'm still number one on your list . . . ?'

If Johnson was surprised to be getting away with it, he was at pains to conceal the fact.

'For the present I want you to stay within the city

jurisdiction. If you try to go outside it you will be instantly arrested.'

The detective who was to tail him, a raw-boned local with prodding dark eyes, had been instructed that coyness was not essential to the contract. From the window they watched him setting out after his quarry – Johnson must have known he was there, although he didn't turn his head.

'I suppose it's all right, sir, to let him go like that . . . ?' All Stephens's uneasiness returned at the sight.

'Come on – let's go to bed! It's getting on for two already, and in the morning we've got a couple of statements to take.'

The hotel into which they had been booked was only a short distance from the marketplace and as they walked there, step for step, they didn't meet a single person. A train whistle from the Thorne Yards was the only sound to break the stillness and above them, in a clear sky, a new moon was scratched in silver.

CHAPTER EIGHT

'SUPERINTENDENT GENTLY.'

'Damn it – you get up early, Gently!'

Gently grinned, snuggling himself a little deeper in his pillows. It was in fact five minutes to eight and he could hear the weather being announced: 'An anticyclone over the Azores is continuing almost stationary . . .'

A cup of tea stood on the cabinet from which he had unlatched the phone, the sun was streaming through the window and the traffic was busy below. From next door, where there was a bathroom, he could hear the comfortable sound of a filling bath; in his imagination he could see the water descending and savour the voluptuous fragrance of bath salts and steam.

'I'm sorry if I got you up . . .'

'My dear fellow, don't waste apologies. Though at this hour in the morning – you remember what Caruso said about it? "Madam, I can't spit . . . !" Well, it's like that with me: I need at least a pint of coffee to turn me into a human being.'

'I'd like to see you later this morning, sir.'

'Then you'll have to come along to my studio, Gently. I'm a professional, you know, not a mewling amateur – I stand to my easel between ten and one.'

Gently chuckled to himself. How the phrase suited Mallows! One could visualize his stocky figure planted, fencer-like, before a canvas. Off-hand he couldn't remember ever having seen a small Mallows picture; they were created for noble rooms and for great carved and gilded frames.

'I'll be along at about eleven if I'm not held up.'

'Good. Will you be on duty, or could you stand a drop of sherry?'

'I'll be on duty . . .'

'Never mind. I promise not to tell a soul. And I suppose it's no use asking what you're digging after now?'

Gently hung up, still chuckling. One couldn't help being taken with Mallows. Mirrored in him, one could perceive a long line of master painters. They were professionals and proud of it! They had no time for self-centred aesthetes. They were the strong, the prolific creators, on whose brushes few doubts ever sat, and they produced those arsenals of work from which the small men and critics dissented.

He had the papers on his breakfast table and found that the Johnson case was overshadowed. The Yard had made their concerted sweep on the information of Herbie the Fence, and at last they had got their hands on Jimmy Fisher's executioner.

★ ★ ★

38 Arrests in Mammoth East End Swoop
Warehouse battle – Constable shot.

In a series of raids carried out last night, Scotland
Yard and the Metropolitan Police virtually wiped out
the rival gangs of East End warehouse bandits. Acting
on a tip-off, they surrounded a warehouse in Poplar.
At the same time swoops were made on premises in
Stepney, Wapping and Whitechapel.

At Poplar, where a gun battle developed, a
constable was shot and seriously wounded. The
gunman was later arrested with five members of his
gang. They are expected to be able to assist the police
in their inquiries into the killing of the notorious
Jimmy Fisher . . .

The Scotland Yard officer in charge of the
operation was Superintendent Pagram, of Homicide.
Superintendent Gently was also working on the case,
but left it yesterday to take charge of the Shirley
Johnson murder.

The raids came as the culmination of long weeks
of arduous routine work . . .

Gently wrinkled his nose and passed the paper across to
Stephens. So they had finally done it: they had laid Jimmy
Fisher's ghost. There was, naturally, a good bit of 'arduous
routine' still to be undertaken, but now it was coasting
home on a downhill gradient; while, if they had recovered
the gun, even that might be abbreviated.

'I'm glad they got around to mentioning your name, sir.'

Secretly, so was Gently; after all, he had earned it! And from the way it was put . . . if you read between the lines . . . All in all, he finished his breakfast in a mood of quiet complacence.

At Headquarters he had to confer with Hansom and Superintendent Walker, two gentlemen who were bound to be critical of the way he had treated Johnson. Unlike Stephens, however, they had precedents to go on, and they warily refrained from open disagreement with Gently.

'It turns out, then, that Johnson has got a rip-snorting motive?'

Hansom couldn't help dotting the i's and crossing the t's.

'You could pull him in at any time, and make a charge stick?'

'At any time I feel that I'm one hundred per cent sure of him . . .'

He left them in the Super's office to talk over his sins, Stephens, in the meantime, having fetched Dolly to make her statement. It amused him to watch Stephens's reactions to the attractive barmaid; aware of his susceptibility, the Inspector became extremely punctilious.

'You appreciate that we have to put it in statement form, miss . . .'

'If you'll be good enough to read it through, miss . . .'

'Yes, miss. Sign it *there* . . .'

In the end it was doubtful who was most impressed by the other – Dolly, it was certain, had an eye for Stephens's good looks. He saw her out through the foyer and they parted in mutual embarrassment. Coming back, he sat thoughtfully silent while his senior brooded over the statement.

'What do you think about Aymas calling Mrs Johnson a liar?'

'Aymas—?'

'Previous to that, they'd been so friendly together.'

Stephens frowned and twisted his fingers. 'She might have been kidding him about his pictures.'

'"Liar" was a strong term to use.'

'Well . . . about another bloke, then.'

There could be no question that they needed to know more about the meeting. It was the thought on which Gently had slept, and which had occasioned his call to Mallows. If you were going to mark time on Johnson, then the meeting became your first object; it was from there that Shirley Johnson had walked to her death, with the accusation of 'liar!' still echoing in her ears. And, out of all those that had been present, it was her accuser who most caught the eye.

'It's a pity that we didn't get something positive from the breakers . . .'

He had seen the report of the detective who had been engaged in the search. The wheels, engine and body of Aymas's car had been identified, but the body had been gutted and crushed in a press. The mats and linings had in any case been destroyed in an incinerator, while the seats and their cushions had been lost among a thousand others. Short of testing the whole pile there was nothing to be done, and even if blood reactions had been found, they could not be tied to Aymas's car.

If Aymas had had something to hide, then he had hidden it with outstanding efficiency.

Butters's Rolls slid up to HQ at a few minutes before

ten o'clock. Butters, in honour of the occasion, wore a black jacket over pinstripe trousers. His buttonhole, almost inevitably, was a large white carnation, and on his head he wore a bowler and on his hands pigskin gloves. His daughter, looking dark-eyed, had also been produced in black; she wore a tailored two-piece suit but its lapel was innocent of flowers.

'As you see, we've come along, sir . . . expect you need my statement too.'

He had been drinking already that morning: you could smell it two paces off.

Gently handed Butters to Stephens, wanting the daughter on his own; but if he had been expecting her to talk more freely he was in for a disappointment. Her mood had changed from that of last night's. The hysterical undertone had been repressed. Now she was very much what she looked, the well-bred offspring of a 'county' family. She sat stiffly upright on the office chair, and neatly folded her hands on her lap.

'Just some questions to start with, Miss Butters . . .'

Gently was consciously using his 'paternal' manner. Instead of facing her across Hansom's desk, he had perched informally on a corner of it.

'I've been talking to your fiancé . . .'

Again, he deliberately chose this term.

'He confirms what you were telling me, especially in relation to Monday night . . .'

But he might as well have saved his guile, because Miss Butters was not to be loosened. She had taken her second wind, as it were, and she was painfully on her guard. Her statement was carefully brief. It was a model of cautious admission. She answered his questions with unresponsive brevity and refused to be cajoled into voluntary additions.

Had she been on the phone to Johnson? Gently knew that he had spent the night at his flat.

'What happened on the Sunday evening?'

'Derek drove us to the cottage. During the afternoon we'd been sailing, and Derek had his tea with us. We said we were going for a spin to the coast.'

'What time did you return to Lordham?'

'At ten p.m.'

'Did Derek go in with you?'

'Yes. He had a drink with father.'

'Was his wife mentioned that day?'

'No, she wasn't mentioned.'

'On the Monday, what did you talk about?'

'About the business, about Thrin Mouth regatta.'

And so it had gone on, from start to finish; you could almost hear the thud as the questions were dead-batted.

'By the way! Touching your phone conversation with Johnson last night . . .'

'There wasn't a conversation. I haven't spoken to him since Monday.'

But at last, after the statement was typed out and signed, a small flicker of emotion did break through the act:

'Is he – is Mr Johnson at the police station now?'

Gently mimicked her flat responses:

'No. He isn't here . . .'

Butters was able to confirm that his daughter hadn't used the telephone – after Gently left there had been a row, and then Butters had locked her in her room. His wife, he admitted, had taken the daughter's part, and on the

128

morrow, which was Sunday, there was a family conference in prospect.

The poor fellow had a stricken look, and perhaps wasn't far from tears.

The hour was closer to twelve than eleven when Gently fetched his Riley from the garage, having previously had a chat with the detective who had done the night shift on Johnson. Stephens, invited to go along, preferred to attend to another angle: he wanted to beat round the car-park area in the hope of flushing a reluctant eyewitness.

'We caught the chummie just like that on the Kenwood case, sir. There was a type who saw the job done, but the locals hadn't got on to him.'

'That was a case in a thousand, Stephens.'

'All the same, sir . . . I'd like to have a shot.'

So Gently had left him to it, and set out to see Mallows alone.

Mallows lived in Oldmarket Road, which was the handsome south-west approach to the city; he also had a Regency house but in the more elaborate, urban style. It stood a good way back from the road and was largely screened by a plantation of beeches. Around this went a double carriage-sweep, its terminals guarded by fine stone gateways. The house itself was faced with plaster. It was designed to give a monumental effect. The lofty centre section was supported by a pair of recessed ones, and in the angles between them nestled two single-storey units. The whole was decorated with moulded plaster, with shallow apses, urns and friezes, and it displayed with the greatest virtuosity the period penchant for wrought-iron ornament.

A small, elderly man answered Gently's ring, and the

detective was ushered up a narrow but gracefully swept stairway. From the landing some plainer stairs departed to the second floor and it was here that, by joining three rooms, the artist had contrived his studio.

'You're late, Superintendent ... who's been going through the mill?'

Mallows had come to the doorway to greet him, his palette and brush still held in his hands. He wore the conventional artist's smock with a beret to contain his rebellious hair. The former, though stained and stiffened with paint, gave the artist an ecclesiastical air.

'Bring us a bottle of sherry, Withers – drop of the '16, I should think. It wouldn't do to offer common stuff to a man like the Superintendent. Oh, and what about stopping to lunch? We've got some fried chicken, with a flan to follow ... Withers, you'd better inform Mrs Clingoe: the Superintendent will be staying for lunch.'

As a matter of fact Gently hadn't assented, but then, he hadn't been consulted either. The matter was disposed of as though it scarcely bore noticing – Mallows wasn't going to bother him to make up his mind on such a trifle.

'Come into the workshop – I've got some things I want to show you.'

Gently followed him into the studio, which smelt strongly of turpentine. Surprisingly the place was cool, though lying directly under the roofs; a row of windows, facing north, were swung horizontally in their frames. Along the inner wall ran a line of racks, most of which were stuffed with canvases. Some other racks, considerably larger, filled one end of the studio from floor to ceiling. Under the windows had been built a bench, and this was equipped with a tool or two; beneath it were drawers, some long and shallow, and there was a complicated stand which took up a lot of the floor space.

It was a friendly, informal and yet efficient place, harbouring none of the mess and clutter often to be found in artists' studios. The canvas on the stand was a large, unfinished seascape and it depicted a number of yachts at the beginning of a race.

'Are you a sailing man, Gently? Those are East Coast One-Designs. It's the start of the Harwich to Ostend race – a friend of mine called Jenkins won it.'

'You are painting this for him?'

'Good heavens no! He couldn't afford it. But he saw that I got the commission, so I'm going to do him a little something. By the way, would you like a portrait?'

'No thanks. I couldn't afford it, either.'

'Not for cash, you silly fellow! I'll knock you one off for a souvenir . . .'

He got rid of his palette and brush and wiped his hands on a scrap of stockinet. Then, picking up a pad and some charcoal, he began to sketch with firm, bold strokes.

'You've got a face that asks to be painted . . . good frontal development . . . ocular benevolence. *You're* a fraud as a detective, you know . . . mouth gives you away, and so does your nose. How in the world did you come to take it up?'

Gently shrugged. How did he, if it came to that?

'You might have made a judge, or a priest or something. But not a detective – it's a sheer waste of human material. Just look at that mouth, and the set of the brows! A doctor, even . . . but not a policeman.'

The topic was making Gently feel uneasy, so that he was

glad when Withers interrupted them with the sherry. About Mallows there was a fearless and unceasing penetration; both his brain and his pencil had a scalpel-like sharpness.

'You like a dry sherry, do you?'

'Yes . . . I prefer it dry.'

'Good, because I don't carry much of the other. But this is a Vino del Pasto, Domecq, '16 – that was the best year for sherry since . . . oh, '82.'

Unquestionably they were drinking a fine and delicate sherry. Gently leant against the bench and sniffed and sipped it with appreciation. Mallows, squatting on a window sill, watched him over considered mouthfuls, and every now and then an elvish twinkle came into his eye.

'So you've come back to me, then!' He was forcing Gently to meet his eye. 'You've taken a sniff at Mr Johnson, and you think that he won't do. Personally speaking, I think you're right . . . as you may know, I've done business with him. He, too, has a mouth with a story . . . then there's his nose: that isn't quite a failure. Yes . . . I think you're quite right . . . you mustn't let Johnson bias your viewpoint.'

'Why do you say: "So you've come back to me"?'

'My dear fellow!' Mallows lofted a shaggy eyebrow at him. 'In the first place the Palette Group enjoys level pegging with Johnson, and in the second, I was the last person to see Shirley alive. Have a little more sherry – the second glass is often the best.'

Gently grunted but permitted his glass to be taken. It was a sherry he would have drunk with the devil himself. Again the two of them sat silently drinking, Gently by the bench and Mallows in the window.

'Let me guess, if I can, a few of the things you want to ask me. From the beginning I've tried to look at this affair as you would . . .'

'Wouldn't it be easier if I asked them?'

'Don't spoil the fun, you moron! Let's reverse the roles for the moment – *I'm* the detective, and *you're* the suspect.'

'All right . . . if it amuses you.'

'Drink your sherry and listen to me.

'To begin with, have you ever been to bed with Shirley Johnson?'

'What does the suspect reply?'

'Remember! You're being me.'

'Very well. I think I may have been, but I'd better be quiet about it.'

'That's good – very good. It's what I expected all along. Now, your wanting to be quiet about it opens up some possibilities. If I think that she's been your mistress, then I think I can see a motive. She's been threatening you, hasn't she – threatening to shop you to her husband?'

'I wouldn't go as far—'

'Wait a moment – here's something better!

'Suppose – just only suppose – that you were infatuated with Shirley Johnson. Now it's not enough to go to bed with her – she must be solely, wholly your own. She has become a symbol to you, the fiery cross of a desperate faith: she will, you think, transform your existence, she will give a substance to your dreams—'

'Now you're laying it on too thick!'

'Drink your sherry – I say, just suppose. We can suppose a thousand things to see if they fit the given facts. Of course, I'm not going to claim that Shirley could inspire Olympian

133

passions – she wasn't a beauty, by any means, or brilliant either, or even good. No, she was drearily psychopathic and trying to sublimate her repressions, which, as you no doubt know, is a lot of claptrap and fundamentally impossible.

'Never mind! Take Shirley for what she was, and no more. In this particular equation it doesn't matter in the slightest. On the other side we'll set another unbalanced personality, a man who has never advanced beyond a certain point of adolescence. X – we'll call him X – probably had an unfortunate childhood, enough to set him dreaming compensatory dreams of greatness; it happens all the time, I know – it's the standard pattern of adolescence; but now and then one finds a psyche that never gets beyond that phase.

'He grows up – his body does, and he acquires a surface shell of maturity. There is an annoying world of reality to which, with reluctance, he has to conform. But underneath there remains the fever, the fear-triggered belief in his greatness: he is a statesman, a general, manqué – a poet, perhaps – perhaps a painter!

'One sees him, absorbed, quiet, perhaps friendly-seeming, but behind his shy smile lies a perpetual frost. His best friend, if he can find one, is a representative of his dream-calling, such a one as he feels may understand his smothered genius. And it may be, that as an amateur, he pursues that calling, at the same time imagining the signs of greatness he is exhibiting. He is modest, of course – that is the mask that hides the dream! – but prouder than a peacock if you scratch him unawares.

'So there's my man, this X, becoming infatuated with Shirley. In her he sees a conductor between his dream and its realization. She is the symbol and the path; through her, he can rise to his full stature. First with her the dream becomes fact, but after her, with all the world. Oh, I know it's a common psychological pattern – but here we are dealing with a critical intensity.

'Now to go back to the other side of the equation, to Shirley Johnson and her peculiar repressions. *She* wasn't obsessed by any delusions of grandeur – hers all belonged to quite a different category. She was homosexual, of that I'm certain, but she didn't happen to possess the courage of her secretions; instead she compelled herself to associate with men – not to bed with them, necessarily, but to dominate and tantalize them.

'She liked to be the queen in a circle of men. She liked to rule their roost, to have favourites, to settle disputes. She plotted and intrigued between the two jealous factions, while remaining herself securely perched upon the fence.

'Could our X have possibly chosen a less amenable subject? My dear fellow, our equation was dynamite from the beginning! We may suppose that to start with she smiled upon his advances – flattered them, teased them, brought his dreams to a pitch of madness. Then he began – isn't it probable? – to propose taking his dreams in earnest. He might want to throw up his job and to have our Shirley run away with him. You can guess her reaction – she would have slapped him down with a bang; she would have used that scathing tongue of hers, scattered his dream house to the winds . . .

'Isn't it an amusing supposition to indulge in over some sherry? By and large it fits the facts – at least, while I'm playing the Superintendent!'

He drank, and Gently drank; it had the air of an unexpressed toast. Mallows turned his glass by the stem to display its exquisite spiral filaments.

'Lace twist . . . these are a pair. I'm rather fond of a bit of glass. I picked these up in that shop in Lynton – you know the place? He stung me a fiver.'

'Am I still playing at being the suspect?'

'Yes, of course. Until we've finished our drink.'

'There's a question you forgot to ask me.'

'Don't tell me! Is Stephen Aymas our X?'

Gently nodded, at the same time reaching for the sketching block. He was rather surprised, then, to find what Mallows had been making of him. Other people had sketched Gently at one time or other, but, allowing for different techniques, they had shown a unanimity in their portrayals. Mallows had found something different, something the others had missed. He had shown Gently looking younger and with a wondering expression in his eyes. Yet it wasn't youthfulness either, but some sort of inner illumination; he had done it by lightening all the tones, by smudging and thumbing away the charcoal.

'So what is your answer going to be to that one?'

'I don't quite know. I don't think it would be Aymas.'

'Too much of an extrovert – yes, I agree. An ambitious soul, mind you, but quite a healthy little monad. He would tell the world his wrongs rather than simmer them over in private.'

'You have your own suspicions, of course?'

'If I have, I don't tell my suspects. Don't forget one important point – you were the last person to see Shirley alive.'

136

'Yes.' Gently laid the sketch down on the bench, undecided whether or not he found it flattering. Twice, now, Mallows had recurred to that point . . . why did he feel the need to emphasize it so much?

'If you like I'll go on with my interrogation – this is a game that ought to be popular at parties! Now consider this carefully: you've been cagey about the meeting. There was more going on there than you admitted to, wasn't there?'

'A good deal more . . . there was a row between Aymas and Mrs Johnson. To be frank, it got to the stage where he was calling her a liar. There was such a row down there that it interfered with a darts match in the bar – and it went on for about an hour. It should have been quite a memorable set-to.'

'You are right, quite right – it should have been indeed.' Mallows showed no surprise at the extent of Gently's information.

'On that basis, perhaps, you could make some suggestions?'

'Don't hurry me, man! I'm on the point of putting some to you. Let me see . . .' He did a miming of intense concentration. 'You admitted, I remember, that the Palette Group had suffered a split. On the one side stood the traditionalists (of whom you yourself are a prominent member), and on the other the modernists, and all that sort of flim-flam.

'Shirley Johnson, you tell me, had a foot in either camp, and by her pictures you couldn't discover if she were biased in a particular direction. Both sides had a claim to her and supplied her with favourites.

'Now, I put it to you that you can tell me what happened that evening.'

Gently slowly nodded. 'I could hazard a guess, I think! It seems to fit that she dropped her neutrality and committed herself, that evening . . .'

'Which is exactly what I suspected: she committed herself to the modernists. It was done in a fit of temper, you can bet your last sou on that. Something had happened to upset Shirley before she ever arrived at that meeting, so she picked a quarrel with Aymas, and after him, with the rest of the tribe.'

'She picked it with him because, being her favourite . . .'

'Just so. He was the one she could hurt the most. It was never a question of artistic conviction, just a wicked talent for finding the rawest spot.'

'And what would you make of her breaking out like that?'

'Ah! The first time, too, after she'd ridden the fence for years. But you mustn't try to quiz a Superintendent, you know – you must leave him alone to add his two and two together. By the bye . . . do you think you could use me at Scotland Yard?'

It may have been the result of the sherry, but they both suddenly found themselves laughing – Mallows, indeed, doubled up with mirth, and had to wipe the tears out of his eyes.

'I've told you everything – everything – haven't I? Everything you were going to ask me! That's the silliest interrogation – and the best – you've ever done!'

'There were one or two other points . . .'

'You devil, Gently! But not before lunch, I shan't permit it. We've had quite enough of cops and suspects – damn it, man, I haven't shown you a single picture.'

There was no calling Mallows to order even if Gently

had wanted to, but the academician had already given him more to chew on than he had expected. What was more, and this was rare with Gently, he felt an affinity with the man; Mallows had charm and more than charm – one felt at home with him in a moment.

'These are things I've done for myself, all the ones you see stored in the racks, and there are one or two early canvases which I didn't sell at the time. One day, I'm going to build a gallery. I want to see them all set out. Some artists can't stand their own pictures – *avec raison*, you'll say, of some contemporaries.'

'Wouldn't you find it a bit . . . overpowering?'

'Not a whit. I've got the devil's own ego. Then it's nice to be able to see the subjects that you've got rid of – you won't have to paint *that* again, or these, or those. You can't guess what a satisfactory feeling it gives you.'

'Don't you enjoy painting, then?'

'It's a bed of thorns, my dear fellow. An artist is the most tormented devil alive. He loathes the sight of a blank canvas and yet he's always standing in front of one – he sees a vision which gets on his nerves, and somehow then he has to get rid of it. Until that's done, he can't live with himself. He's like a prophet with a gag in his mouth. You've heard me say it before, and I'll say it again: either you paint *for* someone, or else you're not an artist; and that goes for every other art under the sun.'

While he spoke he was pulling out one canvas after another, bewildering Gently by the succession of subjects. Unlike most of his contemporaries Mallows scorned to specialize, and his astonishing talents seemed to embrace the entire cosmos. Landscape, seascape, portraiture, still life, each one had come to be conquered by that luminous, rich brush; crowd scenes, architecture, horses, snowscapes, even historical reconstructions; there seemed nothing that he hadn't attempted.

'Do you see what it is I'm trying to do? Good lord, what a period this is for an artist! For years I've been telling people where they stand with art, and might as well have shouted it up a chimney. We've changed our whole footing, that's the point of departure. Without noticing it, we've crashed through a spiritual sound barrier. There's a curtain pulled, Gently, across the centuries preceding us, and it's cut off the old sun to leave us blinded by the new.

'Do you know what engendered art, and society, and everything else? It was fear, plain fear, nothing bigger or nobler than that. Fear of life, fear of death, fear of all the great Unknown: it drove men to get together, to search for a meaning, to increase their stature.

'Just as it did our old friend, X! This was his tragedy, historically foreshadowed. A race of X's were driven together, to glorify themselves and to tame their universe. They insisted that it should be significant and they set up gods who understood it; and then, by pomp and rank and circumstance, they added divinity to man.

'Which was where art came into the picture – its job was to gild the ersatz lily. It had to inject mere nature with significance, and to exhibit man as larger than life. And that, my dear fellow, it was doing, up and down the painful centuries; until a handful of decades ago, art had no other aim at all.'

'But now . . . ?' Gently pressed him hesitantly, painfully conscious of his threadbare ignorance.

'Ah! There's the question which vexes the age – the flywheel has dropped off, and the machine has flown to pieces.

'It happened, as it was bound to, that man came to his senses. It was a long time stirring but it came to a head in the last century. He was in fact growing up, he was throwing away his baubles; he had begun to grasp his universe and himself, and how things worked. So he could do without the gilt, having trampled on the lily. There was scarcely any need for the sublime any longer. The arts, which had always purveyed it, were rapidly stranded high and dry; they had lost their *raison d'être* and they were left with the bleak, flat truth.

'A desperate state of affairs indeed! No wonder it presented a scene of chaos. The tradition of a thousand years was dead, and man was left without a precedent . . .'

'And so you got all this . . . hocus-pocus?'

'Yes. It was every man for himself. Theories, slogans, cranks and abuse – art became a bedlam of heroes and panic. And now, to cap it, there's the "New Criticism", to prove that a couple of blacks make a white.

'If you are faced with an art which is meaningless, why, you proclaim that art shouldn't have a meaning . . .'

At that stage they had returned to the doctrine, and it lasted until Withers called them to lunch; once Mallows had fairly got into the subject he pressed it along like a yacht under full sail.

'My dear fellow, I can lecture all day . . .'

Gently's acknowledging shrug was rueful. But he hadn't been bored during that enthusiastic monologue, and all the while, round the corner, lurked the prospect of fried chicken . . .

But this, unhappily, he was destined never to eat; he was called away to the phone before he had even finished his soup. It wasn't Stephens but Hansom who had made a call so untimely, and there was a mocking ring in the Chief Inspector's voice.

'I thought you'd like to hear how the Johnson boyo was doing. You know, he always struck me as a restless sort of character.'

'How do you mean . . . ?'

'He's done a skip act – bolted – skedaddled out of town. He cleared his bank account at eleven, and that's the last that anyone's seen of him.'

'But what about the tail?'

'Yeah.' Hansom sounded a little sour. 'He fell for the oldest gag in the book – Johnson went in at the front door and came out at the back. That's why it's taken so long to hear about it. Our dumb-bell stood waiting there over an hour. Then he did a quick tour of Johnson's flat and office – all that, before he decided to let us know.'

'You've got an alert going?'

'Yep. Shoot him on sight. And that's not as funny as you think it is, either. You want to know what the boyo was hoarding in his safe deposit? It was a souvenir Luger, with a belt full of ammo!'

Gently clamped down the receiver and swore, far from gently.

CHAPTER NINE

J OHNSON'S RED MG was parked blatantly in front of the
bank, which was a branch in a street only a stone's throw
from his office. A constable stood by it with the
self-conscious air of picketed constables. A police car,
Hansom's, was jammed in behind Johnson's.

'The Chief Inspector is with the manager, sir.'

Gently nodded and strode on in. Behind their counter
with its barricades of varnished mahogany the clerks
glanced quickly, deprecatingly towards him.

'Superintendent Gently . . .'

'This way, sir, please.'

A counter flap was lifted for him, and he was led down
an aisle of desks.

In the office he found Stephens as well as Hansom. The
young Inspector avoided his eye; he had an awkward,
apologetic look.

Hansom quickly took Gently aside:

'This geezer knows more than he's letting on! There's
only one back way out of here, and it goes through the
private hall of the bank house . . .'

'What does he say about it?'

'Says that Johnson was a friend of his.'

The manager was, as Gently had realized, the man he had met in the George III. His smile had now become a little less cordial, but he was still making an effort to keep it in place.

'So . . . we meet again, Superintendent!' He made a wan attempt to sound facetious. 'I didn't imagine that it would have been quite so soon . . .'

Like Stephens, he had an apology in the way he carried himself, but unlike the detective he suffered from no trace of awkwardness. As a senior bank official he understood the airs and graces: he made a slight, ingratiating movement as he felt Gently's deliberate scrutiny.

'Perhaps you'd like to tell me exactly what happened?'

'Certainly, Superintendent. I've just been telling these gentlemen.'

'You're James Farrer, aren't you?'

'Yes, that's my name . . . as you know, I am one of the Palette Group members.'

Gently grunted, his mind switching momentarily to the exhibition. Now he remembered one of the bank manager's pictures – a rather commonplace affair, a still life of roses.

'Johnson was shown in here at eleven or thereabouts. I should tell you that I know him socially, that's to say, he belongs to my club. He informed me that he wanted to close both his accounts – he was in some sort of a crisis; I understood it to be financial.'

'Did he say it was financial?'

'No.' Farrer whipped up his smile. 'But in a bank

144

manager's office one rarely hears of any other kind. In any case, I understood him so . . . I even offered to give him advice. However, he only wanted his money, and it was not my place to question him.'

'Didn't it strike you as being just a *little* bit queer?' Hansom weighed in with his heavy sarcasm.

'It did cross my mind, I have to admit . . . but then, you fellows didn't seem to be worrying about him.'

'You could have stalled him and got on the phone!'

'I'm sorry.' Farrer shrugged his shoulders politely. 'I would certainly have done so had I known he was wanted, but of course, in my eyes, he was still a free agent.'

Gently inquired: 'How much did you let him have?'

Farrer consulted a memo which lay on his desk.

'From his current account, seven hundred pounds . . . and another six hundred against his deposits. That was the best I could do at a moment's notice. In cash, I mean. He wanted small notes.'

'What about his safe deposit?'

'He emptied his box. Naturally, I'm not supposed to know what was in it. Since I advised him about his investments, however . . . if you insist, I can give you a fairly good guess.'

'It might be useful.'

'Well . . . ten or eleven thousand . . . bearer bonds, preference . . . some government stock.'

'And a Luger pistol?'

'Yes, that . . . he once showed it to me.'

'Did he show you his licence?'

Farrer shrugged again, smiling thinly.

'All right – how long was he occupied by these transactions?'

'Not more than half an hour. He was in a hurry – did I say?'

'And then?'

'Well, then he left, after shaking my hand.'

'By the back door – through your hall?'

'It's the quickest way into Shadwell Street.'

'And *of course* – you were friends!' Hansom bit in again. 'And *of course*, you didn't ask him why he was scuttling out at the back! And *of course* he didn't mention that there was a detective watching the front – when we're all so damned polite we don't talk about these things!'

Farrer winced under the attack, but clung to the shreds of his official smile. Too clearly he was a man who couldn't be bullied out of his composure.

'He asked to use that way out as a favour, as he had done once or twice before. It happens to be nearer for his office. I am very sorry if it discommoded you.'

'Yeah, I'll bet you are!' Hansom could detect the delicate taunt. 'But don't think we're so dumb as people make us out, either. There's a little misdemeanour called "obstructing the police", and I wouldn't like to say that we couldn't pin it on you.'

'Always supposing that you had evidence to support it, Inspector.'

Hansom gave one of his snarls, but he knew when he was beaten.

'This money . . .' Gently took up the ball again. 'Can you remember what sort of notes it was in?'

Farrer glanced at the memo. 'Mostly in ones and tens. But I had to give him the odd five hundred pounds in fivers.'

'And you've got a note of them?'

'Yes. They were new and numbered consecutively.'

'We'll have the numbers, please, and all you can remember about his securities.'

That was all there was to it: Gently picked up his hat. But Farrer now seemed to be wanting to add something unsolicited. He fiddled with his memo, smiling once or twice at nothing, then:

'You know . . . I've seen as much of Derek Johnson as most people.'

'What do you mean by that?'

'Oh, just that I thought him fairly trustworthy. We don't come to be bank officials without having a flair for judging character.'

'You're saying that he wouldn't have murdered his wife?'

'Yes . . . no. I don't want to interfere! But I feel it my duty to say that to one who knows him . . . well, it's unlikely.'

For once he wasn't smiling but looking at Gently with an earnest directness, and in a flash Gently understood what the bank manager was trying to convey.

'And you were prepared to back your judgement?'

'The bank is always prepared to back it.'

'It's kind of you to be so frank, Mr Farrer!'

'I think, in justice, I could be no less . . .'

Hansom, as sore as a baited bear, slammed the car door with a fearsome crash. 'It makes my blood simmer – and we can't lay a finger on him! For all we can show it was just the way he tells it – and then the grinning chimpanzee has to go and rub it in!'

Gently closed his door more quietly, though he sympathized with Hansom. On the other hand, one had to spare some admiration for Farrer. The man had stood by his friend at a certain risk to himself, and had risked a little more to impress his faith in Johnson on Gently.

Whatever faults the ex-pilot had, at least he could command a great deal of loyalty . . .

'So what are we going to do about it, besides sitting on our fannies?'

'I'm going to have lunch. You dragged me away from it.'

'But this geezer's got a gun!'

'That's regrettable, of course. But I don't feel any the less hungry because of it.'

Surprisingly, Hansom didn't go up in smoke – he was learning to take his Gently more temperately, perhaps. He extricated the Wolseley with much clashing of gears, but Hansom at his best was no trophy winner with a car.

'I've alerted the rail police and put a man on the bus terminus – and one each, of course, on the office and the flat.'

'You remember young Huysmann?'

'Hell yes! And you were right there. I'll ring up the river police and have them check on the boats. That's it, I reckon, apart from putting out the numbers.'

'Just one other thing . . . he left his car behind.'

'You think—?' Hansom's eyes left the road for a moment.

'We'd better check on it, since he's so flush with the ready. In his place, my next move would have been to buy another car.'

Also, Gently thought, he would have shaved off that moustache, though whether Johnson could have borne to part with it was quite another matter. With him it was probably a gimmick like the chair and the horseshoe, and he would doubtless sooner hang with it than face the world clean-shaven.

'You're not forgetting Miss Butters, sir . . . ?' These were the first words Stephens had spoken; from his behaviour one would have thought that he was personally responsible for Johnson's escape.

'No, I haven't forgotten Miss Butters.' Gently eyed his confrère humorously. 'She's probably the best bet of the lot – perhaps you would like to keep an eye on her?'

Stephens flushed. 'I was going to suggest it . . .'

'Righto, my lad! We'll find you some transport. But remember that Johnson has got a gun . . . If he should turn up, just ring us at Headquarters.'

He had Hansom drop him off outside his hotel, where he went straight down to the below-stair dining room. Being Saturday, the place was crowded in spite of the lateness of the hour, and the waitress who served him looked fagged as well as heated.

'You wouldn't have a plate of fried chicken, would you?'

In the end, he settled for steak with new potatoes and peas. Cramming the tables round about him were red-faced farmers, those who were attending the weekly cattle market that was held beneath the Castle. Watching them, he wondered how many would stray into the exhibition, which, well found in posters, opened directly off their sale ground. Their wives, perhaps, but what about the menfolk . . . ?

He could imagine their reaction to the Wimbush fishes!

After the steak, with which he had drunk half a pint of bitter, he ordered an apple turnover and custard sauce. The noise and clatter of the farmers, whose Saturday lunch was an institution, had a pleasantly lulling effect in the warm and gravy-scented room. As happened so often, his mind relaxed over a meal. It seemed to loosen the ideas that until then were held rigid. Apparently without assistance they began to sort and adjust themselves, forming patterns and suggestions like the pieces in a kaleidoscope.

There was for instance that sketch of Mallows, which lay photographed on his brain – was it merely an hypothesis or had Mallows taken it from life? Did he know of such a man, and know him to be infatuated with Shirley Johnson, or was there another and secret reason why Mallows had suggested this to him?

For a little he toyed with the idea that X had been a self-portrait, given adjustment, naturally, to obscure the resemblance. But no, such an assumption had to be fundamentally impossible; what assurances did Mallows need for his spreading, triumphant genius?

Aymas fitted the description a good deal better, allowing his angry young mannishness to be a case of inversion. Mallows, Gently was convinced, was capable of applying misdirection, and a misdirection of this kind would be characteristic of him. But was Aymas's choler an example of inversion – or the sort of inversion required to satisfy X? Though he had seen little of Aymas, Gently was disinclined to think so; his impression had been of an irritable extrovert who suffered from glands rather than from psychopathic troubles.

Who, then, was next in line – Wimbush? Baxter? Farrer? The latter had a smile, though it could scarcely be called a shy one! Or was it one of the members whom he had yet to meet – or somebody else entirely, beyond the orbit of the Palette Group?

From the way that Mallows had drawn the portrait Gently could swear that it had had a definite subject, and this was the point which kept emerging through the various permutations. It had been sketched with such vivacity, such unhesitating strokes, as though Mallows had long since explored what he described. Thus it followed that X was a familiar acquaintance of Mallows's, or one at least whom he had had good opportunities to observe. Was it his knowledge, then, which had suggested this interpretation of the murder to him, or did he possess some information which more positively indicated X?

If X were indeed a familiar acquaintance, the academician's hedginess was explicable. Unless he was positive that X had done it, he would take pains not to give him away. But his suspicions, however founded, were strong enough in one article: he had wanted to deflect Gently's interest from Johnson, and so had partly shown him his hand. What would have happened if Johnson had been charged? Would Mallows have volunteered information?

Gently tossed off a cup of coffee which had stood until it was nearly cold. Going back again to the beginning, had Mallows some other reason for that hypothesis? As a man he attracted Gently, but that was a bad excuse for passing him over; on another occasion Gently had met an engaging murderer, and nearly made a third on his list of victims. And there was another point which kept reappearing. Mallows was the last person to see her alive. He had tried to make fun of it but it was hard to laugh it away, and a motive of blackmail was more convincing than the most strongly argued psychological theory . . .

Impatiently, Gently thrust this angle into the background. Somewhere, at some time, you had to trust your instinct about people. About Mallows there was something too sane, too balanced – his reaction to attempts at blackmail would probably have been a public lecture.

So, you were left with the conviction that his suggestion was bona fide, and that his X was a serious alternative to the missing Derek Johnson. And the problem remained, where did you begin looking for X? His outward marks a shy smile, and a trail of hopeless paintings. The field seemed to embrace the Palette Group and the whole acquaintance of St John Mallows . . . unless, by the aid of their pictures, one could winnow out some of the former.

From the hotel kiosk he rang HQ:

'You wouldn't have an art expert on the strength, would you?'

'Art expert my foot . . . !' Hansom's disgust was scathing.

'I'd like a really good man.'

'Well, you won't find one here!'

After thinking about it, he referred Gently to a couple of dealers and to the Art School, but neither of these alternatives seemed to promise much on a Saturday. Instead Gently decided he would try his luck unaided – his judgement of pictures was far from professional, but clue in hand, he might ferret out something.

He met a newsboy while crossing the Paddock and stopped to buy a lunchtime paper. It was still the doings of Pagram which overbalanced the front page.

GUNMAN CHARGED WITH FISHER MURDER
37 More Arrests
Yard Make Clean Sweep Of Criminal 'Empire'

Frederick Peachfield, 39, alleged to be a building contractor, was this morning formally charged with the murder of Harold ('Jimmy') Fisher. While resisting arrest during last night's raids he shot and seriously wounded a Metropolitan Police Constable.

Mopping-up operations are still going on and 37 more arrests have been made in the East End. In a statement to the press made by a senior Yard officer, it is claimed that the Warehouse Gangs have been virtually wiped out . . .

The inference was plain though not explicitly stated – they had recovered Peachfield's gun, and it was the gun which had killed Fisher. Nothing else would so have telescoped the 'arduous routine', and have enabled Peachfield to be charged so promptly on the heels of his arrest. He was an open and shut case. He would never pull another gun . . .

The Saturday influx of country people had not been limited to farmers, and the Gardens were much more crowded than they had been the day before. Their *pièce de résistance* was certainly missing – it was still locked away in the Super's office; but the space it left vacant had not been filled, and curiously enough, it exercised a strong attraction. Gently noticed again that most of the patrons were women. It suggested an amusing extension of Mallows's dictum. If art had to be for someone, and that someone was women, then didn't it follow that women were the principal directors of the course of art . . . ?

A good number of the exhibits were now marked with red stars, and Phillip Watts, in his booth, was being kept busy with inquiries. Gently sifted the jostling viewers for a Palette Group member; after a few minutes' hunting, he spotted the angular figure of Baxter. He made his way across to him.

'You're doing a roaring trade, I see . . .'

Baxter turned to examine him distastefully through his steel-rimmed glasses. He was wearing a jacket of chalky tweed over a neat, plum-coloured shirt, with dark worsted trousers and impeccable sandals. He gave an impression of being enormously hygienic, as though he had scrubbed himself with carbolic soap.

'I don't know if you can refer to this as trade . . . sensation, I would call it: a cheap sensation.'

'Anyway, it's selling pictures.'

I am quite aware of that. But I am not convinced that that is entirely the object of the exhibition.'

Gently grinned to himself – he could imagine Mallows's reply to that one! – but it was not his present purpose to start an argument with Baxter. If it was possible he wanted to get the poster artist's cooperation, to use him as a pick-lock to the problem he had before him. And for this it mattered little that Baxter himself might equate with X, since he could equally well serve as a pointer to himself or to another . . .

'I'm just a layman, of course . . . I think I know what I like.'

'That goes without saying. Only an artist knows better.'

'But naturally I get puzzled, faced with a lot of different pictures . . . in a way, they all seem good. You understand what I mean?'

Baxter did, it was plain from his expression, he could see that Gently was a moron; by his opening remark he had betrayed the soul of a shopkeeper. But there was a note of humility in the policeman's approach, and Baxter forbore absolutely to crush him.

'It seems to escape the majority that art appreciation requires training. One does not, by a stroke of brilliance, become a connoisseur overnight. One must learn to judge a painting as a surgeon does an appendectomy – not by the health of the patient but by the skill of the operation.'

Gently nodded his head woodenly. 'I felt there was rather more to it. It's not enough to like a picture . . . you have to know why you shouldn't like it.'

'Simplifying it, that's the point. Your emotional reaction must be set aside. Unless you can train yourself to do that, you will be perpetually floundering in a sea of preferences.'

'So if I like a picture I should reject it?'

'Yes. It's the first step in appreciation.'

Gently nodded more profoundly, his head a little on one side. He really was learning something, his expression seemed to say! Baxter, unmoved, took off his glasses and proceeded to polish them on a scrap of leather; it still seemed touch and go whether he would bother with Gently or not.

'This exhibition here, for instance . . . I can't help feeling lost in it.'

'They are not a difficult collection.' Baxter replaced his glasses severely.

'I can't make up my mind about them . . . those fish, there, take them . . .'

'You mean those planitonal variations which Arthur Wimbush is exhibiting?'

It was a start, however unpromising, and Gently kept Baxter quietly travelling. He quickly learnt, to his mild surprise, that Wimbush was not the crank he had thought him. The reverse, indeed, was true: Wimbush rippled with significance. Each and every one of his fishes was a planitonal triumph. Like the patient, they may have expired, but nothing could fault the appendectomy.

'You would say, then, that Wimbush possesses a fair degree of talent?'

'A rare planitonal cognition. I think you would say that.'

'Isn't he friendly with Mr Mallows?'

'On the contrary, they are unsympathetic.'

Gently made a mental cross against the name of Arthur Wimbush.

They passed on to Shoreby, with whom Baxter was more censorious. He pointed out traces of involuntary emotion which were marring that gentleman's work.

'With geometrical panels one must preserve discipline; there should be no undercurrent of excitement, either in grouping or brushwork. You can see for yourself how those triangles pulsate, while the parallelogram is tantamount to a slap in the face. Until he is more mature, Shoreby should leave geometry alone.'

'He lacks talent, perhaps?'

'I disagree. He lacks control.'

On the other hand, he was notably friendly with Mr Mallows . . .

In one way Baxter was showing a scrupulous justice: he had sunk his partisan feelings in a desire to educate Gently. Impartially he treated with the concrete and the abstract, letting nothing of his bias interfere with the lesson. He chided Aymas for the unbridled sensuality of his colour – praised Lavery, in spite of his clumsy-looking splurges; he allowed talent to Farrer, though hampered by bourgeois sentiment, and found planic sensitivity in Allstanley's wirework. The difficulty lay in getting a comparative judgement from him. All his geese were to be swans for the necessity of the moment. It was Gently's business as a layman to consider the mechanics of appreciation; the estimation of degrees of talent did not lie within his province.

'I was looking through the pictures that Mrs Johnson painted . . .'

Baxter was 'whiffing' his stalk-like pipe, making successions of quick popping noises.

'Oh? Then you noticed the subliminal approach, I suppose, and the regressional tendency towards prenatal cognition?'

'I noticed erotic fantasies in medieval trappings.'

Baxter looked surprised. 'You could put it like that.'

'Would you say that *she* had talent?'

Baxter whiffed. 'She had emotive power. But it was probably entirely posited on a disassociated psyche.'

'Sexual frustration, to put it bluntly?'

'Y . . . es. It's safe to say so.'

'And was she the only group member with a psychopathic motivation?'

Baxter looked a little startled, but he still kept popping away.

'I hadn't thought it before, though of course, you may be right.'

'Could you give me any suggestions?'

'No, I don't think so. Not at the moment. It's an entirely new conception, and I would need to give it some thought. What put the idea in your head?'

'Oh, just a general curiosity about painters.'

'It's possible that you've hit on something – I must really consider the matter.'

Now, instead of drawing him out, he had shut Baxter up. The artist seemed to have nothing more that he wanted to say to Gently. His back leant against a booth, he stood whiffing on and on at his pipe, his eyes far away above the heads of the passing viewers. Gently watched him for a little, equally silent, then he grunted and turned away.

His round with Baxter hadn't been completely fruitless, nevertheless, since he had got from him a fair idea of how the group members stood with Mallows. There were five who were friends of his, outside the group, and if X was a group member then this quintet was likely to contain him. On a page of his personal notebook he scribbled down these five possibles adding, as was his habit, what seemed most relevant about each of them:

[1] Stephen Aymas. Paints gooey landscapes with some success. Noisy, extroverted. Mallows thinks he will make the grade.

[2] James Farrer, bank manager. Seems a good man at his job. Paints chocolate-boxy flowers. NB Would Mallows think his smile *shy*? NNB Shouldn't think Aymas smiles much.

[3] Frederick Allstanley. Still to meet him. Sculpts mainly in wire. Elementary schoolteacher (grounds for delusions of grandeur?).

[4] Jack Seymour. Pal of Aymas's. Paints minutely

worked still lifes. Shy, with shy smile. But only in middle twenties.

[5] Henry Baxter. Pedant. Rather secretive. A professional (and successful) poster artist. Another non-smiler (was Mallows truthful about smile?). NB Does Baxter feel frustd. painting posters? NNB Does he paint anything else?

There were small grounds for optimism in this varied group of possibles, unless Allstanley turned out to be the living image of Mallows's description. By the car test Aymas was the number-one candidate, but Gently felt less and less inclined to value that theory. There had been no need for a car to have been left on the park. It was enough to represent it there to lure Shirley into the darkness. But it had needed a person who was known to have a car, and this seemed to eliminate Seymour, his gratifying shyness notwithstanding.

Over the remaining two names Gently pondered narrowly. Against Farrer, of course, a black mark already stood. With more or less culpability he had assisted Johnson to escape, which, if he were guilty, it was in his interest to do. Unfortunately his qualifications seemed to end there. He was a success in his profession and it fitted him like a glove. He painted badly, it was true, but there was nothing to show that he took painting seriously; the city had an artistic climate and suggested daubing as a hobby.

This left him with Baxter, his non-smiling pedant, whose head was stuffed with jargon and critical theory; a man the complete antithesis of the brilliant and fertile Mallows – if you liked, the born failure, as against the born succeeder! Of him one could readily believe an inner frustration, a delusion of greatness that smouldered in neglect. *Now* he was merely a poster artist, but some time, when he would, he could burst through that disguise and blaze his name to the high heavens . . . perhaps, when Shirley Johnson became his worshipping mistress. Yes, one could believe it of the nervously whiffing Baxter: it needed only the conscious smile – and wouldn't that have been lost on Monday night?

Gently snapped shut his notebook and pushed his way across to the booth. There, temporarily free of inquirers, Watts was adding up some figures on a pad.

'Are you making plenty of hay?'

'Yes, sir! This is our best . . . our best ever. Even Arthur Wimbush . . . I really think we're going to sell out . . . !'

'Have you sold Mr Baxter's poster?'

'Yes, sir. I saw you talking to him . . .'

'Doesn't he paint anything else besides posters?'

'Oh yes, sir. He paints landscapes too.'

'Hmn.' Gently appeared to meditate the point. 'Has he done anything that might suit a detective's den?'

'Well, sir . . .' Young Watts was equally thoughtful. 'He's done a fine view of the Heath with a prospect of the prison . . .'

'Good is he – apart from these posters of his?'

Watts flushed. 'I don't think . . . I couldn't say, not really. He usually sends several things to the exhibition . . . I believe they think that he's best at posters.'

So that was Baxter lined up behind the absentee Johnson, with, in a manner of speaking, Allstanley still to play. But to them one was obliged to add an unlimited number of outsiders, since suspicion could not be confined to the group members alone.

On returning to Headquarters he found, already, a message from Stephens:

'Couldn't we have the phone tapped? I've seen her using it, I think . . .'

This conjured up a picture of Stephens lurking among the laurels, and trying to stifle a treacherous sneeze as the gardener passed by him.

Hansom, who had taken the tip about checking on car purchasers, had so far only uncovered a minor misdemeanour.

'A chummie with an expired licence bought a car and drove it home . . .'

He seemed to take it much to heart that they hadn't immediately grabbed Johnson.

Gently arranged for Stephens's relief and then departed again for Glove Street. The manageress, treating him now as a regular, found him a table beside the window. Most of the patrons had evening papers in which they were reading of Pagram's triumph, but the local titbit, Johnson's flitting, had been temporarily placed under wraps.

Beyond Glove Street, in St Saviour's, one heard the weekend exodus in motion, and several patrons were claiming suitcases when they went to pay their bills.

CHAPTER TEN

No CALLS HAD been put through to the hotel during the night, and Gently heard nothing about the slashings until he checked in at Headquarters.

The morning was dull and uncommitted, promising neither sun nor rain; it was a morning when you didn't much care whether you were stuck in the city or out of it. Stephens he had seen the evening before, and the Inspector was gone again before Gently got up. After the degenerate custom of Elphinstow Road, he had ordered his breakfast to be sent up to his room.

There, among the pillows, he had disembowelled the papers, making them greasy with his buttery fingers; then, feeling irritable and inclined to a headache, he had taken himself off to a tepid shower.

Up here, the Sundays were so intensely sabbatical! In place of traffic one heard the chirping of sparrows under the eaves. And there were huskily crooning pigeons in the elm trees beneath the Castle, and the weird, unanalysable cries of an itinerant news vendor.

While dressing he had looked through his window into

a street completely deserted; there wasn't even a Sunday stroller where a traffic jam had been yesterday. He was tying his tie when he caught sight of the first pedestrian, and then it was a bus conductor on his way to the terminus. As for cars! Well, a couple of them were parked across the way, but there was nothing else in that line except a locked and deserted motor coach.

Not until he reached the marketplace did he discover a semblance of life. Here some corporation employees were hosing down the numerous gangways. The water had spread across the Walk, bearing litter and shavings with it, and there was a smell of damaged fruit and an echoing grate of shovels. A shabby old man stood furtively watching . . . was it the same one who had discovered the body? Suddenly he dived into the heap of rubbish, producing a coin which he rubbed on his sleeve . . .

Hansom had also bought a sheaf of papers and he was digesting them in his office. He was chewing a short, black cheroot, his favourite form of nicotine ingestion.

'Well, I found that car dealer for you!' He tossed a report sheet across the desk. 'He flogged Johnson a nice quiet '53 Minx – a bit of a change from MGs, isn't it?'

Gently took up the report sheet and glanced over it, shrugging. A Minx was an obvious choice for Johnson. It was a car as unobtrusive as any car could be: the unregistering norm, a car to go unnoticed.

'You've put it out, have you?'

Hansom ringed him with cheroot smoke. 'We made it an all-stations, because where the hell is he by now? Not in Northshire, that's a safe bet, and maybe not in England either. But my guess is that he headed straight for the Smoke.'

'When did you find this car dealer?'

'Just this morning, like it says.'

'Any message from Stephens?'

'Nope. His relief is in the canteen.'

Gently went to talk to the relief, who was sombrely eating a canteen breakfast. The man had spent a tranquil night and had nothing of interest to report. Previously, as Stephens had told Gently, Butters's family had arrived in two cars; lights had been burning when Stephens was relieved and had continued to do so until past one a.m.

'Did you see any traffic go past the house?'

'Not till seven, when the milkman got there.'

'You had a good look at him, did you?'

'Yes. He was a young fellow; short; dark brown hair.'

It was five minutes later, when Gently was back in Hansom's office, that the desk sergeant buzzed to say that Baxter wanted to see them. He was shown up straight away and he arrived strangely breathless; his glasses were held in his hand, which added to his distrait appearance.

'I've just come from the exhibition – run all the way . . . !'

He brushed aside Gently's suggestion that he should take a seat.

'No, this is serious – deadly serious, you understand? That fellow – that barbarian Johnson! He's slashed all the paintings!'

'Johnson!'

Hansom was on his feet in a moment. From the beginning, one felt, he had looked on Johnson as personal meat.

'You've seen Johnson around?'

'No . . . don't be silly! But he's slashed them with the knife – the same one. It's still there!'

164

A minute or two of careful questioning was required to get the facts from him. For once he had been rattled out of his disdainful sang-froid. He stuttered and gestured and stared with his naked eyes, too upset, apparently, to clean and replace the smeary glasses.

'I – I . . . this morning I had to go there – Watts gave me the key – on Sundays it's closed . . . the exhibition, I mean! And that's how I found it – slashed, every one of them! The glass all broken . . . the knife stuck in a frame . . .'

'Just a minute! What were you doing at the exhibition this morning?'

'I . . . well, if you must know! I went to touch up my exhibit . . .'

'And where does Johnson come into it?'

'He . . . isn't it too obvious? It's his revenge, because he thinks that one of us killed his wife . . .'

Hansom was watching Baxter curiously, and now he shot a look at Gently. Gently shrugged, looking wooden, but he understood his colleague's hint.

'Well . . . we'd better go and look at it. Did you lock the gate after you?'

'Yes – no, I can't remember! I ran all the way . . .'

He had entered the Gardens by the gate at the rear, the one which gave access to Market Avenue. Here, as at the provision market, men were busy with brooms and hoses, and in the air lingered the musky smell of animal occupation. Baxter's Singer stood alone by a granite horse trough. It was a pre-war ten with rather dubious tyres. He had not locked the gate, which was secured by a chain and padlock, and in fact it stood ajar with the key still in the lock.

'Holy smoke . . . just look at this!'

A single glance took in the havoc. It was as though a malicious child had been let loose among the pictures. Raw destruction, it was just that, the very sight of it kindling anger. Profoundly shocked, one could only feel enraged at the insensate author of it.

'That's just how I found it . . . I didn't touch a thing . . .'

Faced with it, Gently could better appreciate Baxter's distraction. They weren't masterpieces, perhaps, those scored and tattered canvases, but they were the products of civilized people patiently cultivating their talents. And now, in an hour of savagery, they had been brainlessly destroyed. It was the treachery that hurt: one felt that something had been betrayed.

'You see? It couldn't have been one of us . . .'

That was true: such a thing seemed unbelievable. An artist might conceivably have mutilated another's picture, but unless he were completely crazed he could never have stooped to this barbarity.

Silently they moved along the line of damaged exhibits, each one of which had been separately, conscientiously attacked. Canvases hung in ribbons, glass lay shattered under empty frames, Allstanley's 'Head of a Laughing Woman' was stamped out flat beside its pedestal. It seemed the work of some berserk gorilla which had been trained in the arts of destruction. One couldn't comprehend the mind behind it; the single reaction was of seething anger.

'Where's that knife you talked about?'

'Here, look . . . at the end. Stuck in this stupid thing of Farrer's – he didn't think it was worth a slash.'

There was no mystery about the knife – it was the fellow

166

of the murder weapon; the same triangular sliver of stainless steel, stamped with the name of the Sheffield cutler. It had been driven hard into the frame of the picture, deliberately cutting through the artist's name. The canvas of this one had escaped a hacking but the force of the blow had wrenched the frame from its brackets.

'Do you remember if you touched the knife?'

'I . . . yes, I may have done. I honestly don't know. I was too upset.'

'Why did you touch it?'

'I don't know if I did or not! I'd read about the other one, and felt certain that this was the same.'

Hansom murmured to Gently:

'Do you want my theory? Chummie's got it in for Farrer for helping Johnson to get away. That's why he got the knife instead of having his picture slashed . . . let's show it to him and watch his face. I'll bet he doesn't grin this time!'

Carefully, Gently disengaged the picture, turning it to the light to examine the knife. There were apparently no prints on the polished metal, and apart from some hack marks, the knife looked new.

'Did any picture of that knife get published?'

'Yeah – or of one just like it. The local carried it, and so did the *Echo*.'

So that anybody, besides the murderer, might have committed this outrage.

'What happened to you after I saw you yesterday?'

Baxter had calmed himself now and had cleaned and put on his glasses. It was surprising what a difference those round lenses made to him; at once, from being a harassed owl, he began to be his contemptuous self.

'I really don't see what that has to do with it.'

'Never mind! I'd like you to answer the question.'

'Very well – I had my tea, and then I drove out to Floatham. I made a sketch of the mill there for a poster I have commissioned.'

'What time did you go to tea?'

'At six, or soon after.'

'When the exhibition closed, in fact?'

'I am not trying to conceal it.'

'And that, of course, would be when you borrowed the key from Watts?'

'Exactly.' Baxter sniffed. 'Your deduction is keen, Superintendent.'

'So it seems that you had the key from around six p.m. yesterday evening?'

'I did. And I have no worthwhile alibi to offer you.'

'You finished your sketch and then went home?'

'To my cottage at Dunton. Where I live by myself.'

'And that is the only key?'

'It's the only one we have, though I dare say you'll find some others if you inquire at the Castle.'

Abruptly Gently left them and stalked out of the Gardens. Across the Avenue they were still hosing pens and forking up the soiled straw. He picked on the driver of the lorry:

'When did you get here this morning?'

They began at seven, he was told, but they had seen nobody in the Gardens.

'When did that Singer park there?' This they hadn't precisely noticed, but a consensus of their opinion was that it hadn't been there for long. One of the sweepers had seen Baxter come out. They couldn't recall any suspicious noises. A number of people had gone by, mostly transport workers, but the only wheeled traffic had been bicycles and a truck.

He returned to the Gardens to find Hansom at work on Baxter – a classic example of bludgeon versus rapier. If anything the artist seemed to be enjoying the contest, and small head tilted, chose his stinging ripostes deliberately.

'You will notice, I trust, that my own picture has suffered . . . ?'

Gently ignored him, drawing the Inspector aside. 'We'll have to treat this as serious though it may be only a hoax – some person with a grudge, who likes to make things spectacular! I'm afraid we'll have to rope in a lot of people. It's going to be a day of old-fashioned routine . . .'

'Do you think it could be Johnson?'

'No. That doesn't make sense. If there's any link at all, it's in the exception made of Farrer.'

'Yeah – that's my impression. Chummie doesn't like Farrer.'

'We'll look him over first, after you've set the wheels turning.'

Farrer was a family man; he had a teenage son and daughter. It was the latter, clad in a dressing gown, who admitted the policeman into the bank house. Here there was an air of Sunday mornings, of relaxation and petty carelessness. One smelt some bacon being fried and saw, on a table, last night's cups. They were taken into the lounge, the curtains of which had to be hastily drawn, while the chairs pushed together in a semicircle suggested that the family had been watching TV.

'I'll just see if Daddy is out of the bathroom . . .'

The girl went out quickly, clutching her dressing gown together. A minute or two later her brother peered in, found a paperback western and retired without speaking.

'It must be nice to manage a bank!' Hansom prowled round the room, allotting price tags to the contents. He was particularly struck by the TV and by the voluptuous Persian carpet. It was a room without taste, however, and overcrowded with oppressive furniture; the walls were hung with some insipid watercolours and the light bowl was of mottled glass.

'Daddy will be with you in just a minute . . .' This time it was Mrs Farrer who came to look them over. She was a heavy, dowdy woman and had prominent brown eyes, and seeing her, one at once understood the room.

'You won't keep him, will you? We're driving over to Lynton . . .'

She brought a smell of bath salts with her, and like the others, wore a dressing gown. Seeing the cushions still awry, she deftly shook them and set them straight. Then she piled the cups together, smiled uncertainly and went out.

Finally, Farrer made his entrance – by way of contrast, neatly dressed. He came forward with his manner of a man who was used to handling business.

'Something new about Johnson, is it?'

He smiled engagingly from one to the other; nevertheless, one could tell from his eyes that he was far from feeling at ease.

'No . . . this is a little different. It's to do with the exhibition.'

'I don't know much about that, I'm afraid.'

'Would you care to tell us how you spent last night?'

After a pause he told them, without any hedging. He had been to his club for a game of tennis. Then he had returned home to watch the television, and had gone to bed soon after it closed down.

'What time did you get up this morning?'

'Oh . . . about nine. Does it matter?'

Now he was beginning to look visibly unhappy, his smile becoming fixed and without conviction.

'Perhaps I'd better tell you what happened.' Gently briefly related the facts. Hansom, sprawling in an easy chair, kept his hard eyes fixed on the bank manager. And he had been right, quite right about one thing: Farrer's smile was not proof against this. Before Gently had done, the last vestige had vanished and a look of unmistakable fear had replaced it.

'So it looks very much as though someone . . .'

'My God!' Farrer had turned almost grey. The shock, indeed, had exceeded Hansom's estimate; it seemed to have dealt a mortal blow to the man.

'I wouldn't be too alarmed . . . it may be coincidental—'

'No!' Farrer's head shook with exaggerated insistence.

'You don't think it is?'

'My God – I know it isn't! You don't know the half of it . . . the other half is here!'

He touched his breast with his hand as though making a dramatic gesture, then, without any warning, he flopped down in a chair. He was shaking so badly that he could hardly get to his wallet. Muscles twitched in his face and at the corners of his eyes.

'It's a nightmare . . . I don't know . . . I wasn't going to show it to you! It was a joke, I thought . . . just somebody taking the rise. I found it this morning. They had shoved it through the door . . . My God – but now! I don't know where I am . . .'

He had managed to get from the wallet a carelessly opened manilla envelope, and this he held out tremblingly for Gently to take. Inside it was a folded sheet of softish grey paper, to one side of which had been pasted some printed capitals:

YOU HELPED HIM TO GET AWAY
THERE'S ANOTHER KNIFE WAITING

They were all of one typeface and had been very neatly arranged. The envelope was a common one such as are sold by the thousand, but the paper was unusual, seemingly of linen manufacture.

'It's a nightmare, I tell you . . . !'

The bank manager's voice sounded hoarse. He made an attempt to get up, then sank back weakly in his chair.

'What have I done to deserve it . . . nothing! I've done nothing at all. He's a madman, whoever it is . . . I want protection until he's arrested!'

Gently passed the missive to Hansom, handling it carefully by its edges. He stared for a moment at the appealing face on which blank terror was stamped so plainly.

'Another time you may not be so ready to fool the police!'

'But I didn't – I didn't know – he didn't tell me you were watching him!'

'Someone thinks you knew, by the look of that letter.'

'But it's a mistake, a crazy mistake! You've got to give me police protection . . .'

Gently shrugged. 'In that case, perhaps we can have your cooperation – you must admit that up till now it hasn't been a conspicuous feature.'

'I'll tell you anything you want to know!'

'Right – what precisely did Johnson tell you?'

'He said that he had to get out for a bit – there was nothing else, I'm willing to swear it!'

'Didn't he tell you who he thought had done it?'

'He asked me that. He thought it was one of us.'

'And what was your opinion about it?'

Farrer swallowed, pointing falteringly at the letter. 'I was certain of that from the first – it had to be one of us who'd done it. Aymas, he was the one I bet on . . . they'd had a flaming row that evening . . .'

'And the letter seems to confirm it?'

'Good Lord! Haven't you noticed what paper it's on? That's a special watercolour paper . . . at first, I told you, I thought it was a joke . . .'

Gently reached for the letter again and examined the sheet of paper closely. It was certainly of an uncommon type, a class of paper he had rarely met with. Though soft and thin, it had the appearance of strength and the surface was finely grained. Held up to the light it showed part of a watermark – a piece of design, with the letters: O . . . DA . . . VI.

'Do you know what sort of paper this is?'

'Of course! I've made a study of papers. That's an Italian one, the "Leonardo da Vinci" – supposed to be the same as da Vinci used.'

173

'Where can you buy it over here?'

'I don't think you can, unless they have some in London.'

'Have you seen any of the members use it?'

'No . . . I've only seen it in reference books.'

Gently lingered a little over the panicky bank manager – just then, he was wanting to be especially helpful! The rest of the bank house was suspiciously silent, and one wondered if some surreptitious eavesdropping was in progress.

'Your wife tells me that you are driving over to Lynton today . . . ?'

Farrer shuddered involuntarily. 'We were going to visit her people . . .'

'It might be wise to postpone the trip.'

'I'm not stirring a foot till you've got him inside!'

Rather against Hansom's wishes, Gently agreed to the police protection – Hansom was thinking more in terms of manpower than of scared bank officials. When the door closed behind them he gave vent to his ill humour:

'On top of all the rest we'll need a whole bunch of search warrants!'

That was the case – interrogations were unfortunately now not enough. Because of the letter they would have to search for incriminating evidence. For some more of that paper, for the source of the printed characters – on the very slim chance that neither of these had been destroyed.

'What's the betting that we don't get a print off that letter – not apart from yours and mine, and the boyo's back there?'

Hansom leant on the Wolseley's wheel and brooded

darkly over the problem; he wore a sub-Byronic scowl when he felt that things were piling up on him.

'There wasn't one on the knife . . .'

'Not on either of the knives! This is a very slick chummie, and he doesn't make mistakes. I can tell you something, though.'

'That it lets Johnson out?'

'Well, doesn't it?' Hansom gave Gently a challenging leer.

'You can take it either way . . . there's somebody who wanted Johnson nailed – or there's Johnson, setting up an Aunt Sally for us to shy at.'

'How do you explain that precious paper?'

Gently grinned. 'Didn't it seem familiar? I've got an impression that you've been nursing a sheet in the office for three days.'

'Hell's bells!' Hansom stared at him. 'Surely not the "Dark Destroyer"?'

'We'll need to check it to be certain, but I'm offering you three to one . . .'

At Headquarters both their guesses were tested and found correct: the letter bore no additional prints and its paper matched that of the picture. It went a stage further. The letter and picture corresponded. The partial water-mark on the one was found completed on the other. The original whole sheet had been divided – by the blade of a sharp knife; the picture represented one half, and from the other had come the letter.

'So what do you make of that? She didn't send that letter herself!'

And if Shirley Johnson hadn't sent it then it followed that her husband had: it was too fanciful to suppose that

175

any outsider had obtained the paper. But her husband, looking for something to simulate a Palette Group origin, would naturally choose a piece of such an arty-looking paper. Therefore he had composed the letter, and therefore he had done the slashing – a piece of deliberate misdirection which could hardly have been conceived by innocence.

Or by sanity, if it came to that . . . though Johnson had seemed to have his wits about him.

'I'd like to know where she got that paper . . . I didn't see any more of it at the flat.'

'I'll send a kiddie out there to look. Perhaps Johnson put a match to the rest of it.'

'There's also another possibility – she might have been given it by one of the others. Maybe just that single half-sheet, it being a difficult paper to come by.'

'Ah-ah!' Hansom shook his head. 'I'm getting cheesed with all these hunches. For me, this fixes it square on Johnson, and that's the way I'm going to see it from now.'

'All the same, we'll go through with the search.'

'Yeah – who are we to rest on Sundays?'

'Every Palette Group member without exception – including St John Mallows. Him, I'll see personally.'

He got on the phone to the academician, who listened without comment while Gently told him what had happened.

'It's a bit of a shock, Gently . . . I don't know what to say.'

'If you will, I'd like you to meet me in the Gardens.'

It was midday and the city had woken up to its Sunday life – there was a thin movement of traffic and a scattering of pedestrians. Many of the latter were church-goers, dressed in sombre, scented decency, in contrast to the scantily clad cyclists who pedalled intently towards the country. From the direction of Thorne Station came the thud of drums and the tooting of bugles, for it was there that the naval cadets had moored their flagship, an ex-MTB.

By now a small crowd had gathered outside the Gardens, and saunterers were peering hopefully through the railings and herbage. A reporter and his photographer were arguing with the constable in charge, but on the appearance of Gently they hastily transferred their eloquence.

'Our editor's getting in touch . . . surely we could take a couple of pics?'

Under the plane trees near the pens the scavengers lingered, a watchful group.

St John Mallows drove up with all the consequence that was dear to him, waving the crowd away from the gate to make a space for his shiny Daimler. He was dressed very sprucely and wore a magnificent bowler hat, and willingly posed by the car to enable the photographer to get a picture.

'Never miss a chance of a press puff, my dear fellow . . . !'

He steered Gently through the gate as though he had personally taken charge of the business. Then he continued to walk briskly, his hand on Gently's arm, paying no attention to the ruined pictures until they were round the bend and out of sight. There he came to a sudden halt and, planting his feet, stared about him.

'Vandalism . . . the purest vandalism!' He snuffed the air as though it contained a fragrance. 'Exhilarating, isn't it? –

because it's so thorough! Just imagine him, will you, as he went round that lot – imagine the pure ecstasy of soul-glutting hatred!'

This wasn't quite the reaction that Gently had expected, but one could predict very little about Mallows's reactions. With his blue eyes sparkling he seemed to be drinking in the spectacle – it held for him a quality transcending moral judgements.

'Unbalanced, of course – psychopathic in capitals – ordinarily, we repress the lust to commit mayhem. But the glorious scope of it – what a masterpiece of catharsis! I don't remember ever having seen such a completely successful blow-up.'

'It's a good job you weren't exhibiting.'

'My dear Gently, don't be petty! This is an occasion on which any man would gladly sacrifice a canvas. I almost wish I'd had one in – feel I haven't been represented. Can't you sense the stupendous energy, the crackling flame of the fellow's loathing?'

'What do you recommend then – an associated membership?'

'Dear me, no! I'm afraid you'll have to lock him up. He's right round the bend, he needs a holiday from life.'

'And who do we happen to be talking about?'

'Why – X. Who else comes into it?'

Farrer's exhibit had been removed along with the knife, and Gently made no reference to this interesting feature. Instead, he quietly produced the letter from his pocket. He offered it to Mallows without prefacing an explanation.

The academician, after glancing at him, unfolded the grey sheet, which he examined without the slightest alteration of expression. After feeling the paper between his sensitive fingers he raised it to the light to look for the watermark.

'Hmm . . . letters were cut from *The Times*, I should think.'

'You take *The Times*, do you?'

'Of course – though I don't read it.'

'What about the paper?'

'It's a flashy Eytie stuff – no good for anything except to hang in the toilet.'

'Where can you get it from?'

'Nowhere, in perfidious Albion. But it's common enough abroad, especially in Italy, where they make it.'

'Have you seen any of the Palette Group with it?'

'No . . . but they might have seen me. I bought some sheets in Verona, just to give the stuff a trial.'

Gently was suddenly aware that Mallows was eyeing him whimsically, his two demonic eyebrows lifted rather like horns.

'Go on, you old bloodhound – now ask me if I did this letter!'

'I was going to ask you something else. To whom did you give a sheet of that paper?'

'Hah!' Mallows made a ludicrous weaving motion with his shoulders. 'You're pretty certain, aren't you, that I know who did it? Well, I've drawn you his portrait to the best of my ability – and now I can look you in the eye and tell you I gave that paper to nobody!'

'Not even to Mrs Johnson?'

'No – and I know what you're getting at. She erupted her "Dark Destroyer" on to a piece: I noticed it when we were doing the selection.'

'And you didn't give it to her?'

'No, Positively not. Nor to anybody else – so there's your answer to the Clue of the Paper.'

Gently took back the paper and tucked it away with the ghost of a shrug. Was Mallows being the slightest bit overemphatic? It wasn't easy to read his lively countenance; it was full of expression, but of expression under command. One suspected that very little slipped past it unawares.

'Now I'll do a little guessing. There's a connection here, isn't there? You found something here that put you on the trail of the letter. Otherwise you might have missed it, he might have kept it to himself. If I read that letter aright, he assisted – Johnson, was it? – to escape.'

'It didn't necessarily refer to Johnson.'

'My dear fellow! Who else is there? He assisted Johnson to elude your clutches – you were shadowing him I suppose? And there's this X, he didn't like it, and it brought on another outburst. He left something here that was threatening to Farrer, and sent him that letter to make it plain . . .'

Gently felt himself grow cold. He had said not a word about Farrer! Deliberately, he had kept the name of the bank manager out of it. He stared unbelievingly at Mallows, and Mallows at him: they were both instantly conscious of that revealing blunder. Then slowly, rather sadly, Mallows began to shake his head.

'I talk too much – don't I? It's always been my downfall . . . But you'd be a fool to attach too much importance to it, you know. To tell you the truth, Farrer rang me this morning – he was worried about Johnson and wanted to confess it. So it wasn't too difficult to deduce that it was he who received the letter.'

A perfectly logical explanation – but the damage had been done. The playful intimacy that existed between them seemed to have felt the touch of a frost. Mallows stood biting at his lip and gazing down at one of the pictures. Gently, hands stuffed in his pockets, wore the most wooden of his expressions.

'There are a few routine questions I have to put to you . . . and naturally, we're making a thorough investigation.'

'I understand that. Damn it, you've got to be thorough. I don't suppose you like it any better than we do . . .'

But he went through the rest of it as quickly as he could, and Mallows confined himself to giving straight answers. He had spent the evening in his garden, and then gone to bed to read; like Gently, he had had his breakfast in bed that morning.

Gently watched him drive away, and then went straight to a phone box. In the directory he found the number of the bank house.

'Superintendent Gently . . . did you ring Mallows this morning?'

Farrer began with a little hedging, trying to find what the query was about.

'I can check with the exchange. I merely thought you'd save me the trouble.'

'I see . . . yes . . . no, I haven't rung him today.'

Gently clamped the receiver down hard on its rest. He remained there, leaning on it, for several minutes.

CHAPTER ELEVEN

H<small>E ABANDONED HIS</small> plan of lunch at his hotel and returned instead to have it in the canteen. Hansom, who was a bachelor, made a habit of lunching there, and had a small, sacred table and even aspired to a private napkin. With this tucked under his chin he had a somewhat ogreish appearance.

'Your playmate rang in – two of the Butters's went to church, the mother and the eldest daughter, in the eldest daughter's car. Then the old man came out and had a mooch around the lawn. He'd been sinking it, apparently, wasn't too steady on his pins.'

'Did nobody else visit the house?'

'No . . . half a mo', the paperman.'

Gently grunted into his soup, imagining the Sunday scene at Lordham. Stephens had taken with him a folding stool of the type familiar to fishermen. His car being concealed, he would have crept to some hedge or shrubbery, and there, with his glasses, have zealously watched the house and grounds. Then, stealing some hasty minutes, he would send his report back on the car's radio, all the time in a frantic rush in case he were missing the vital moment. To be amused by that sort of thing one needed to be as young as Stephens . . .

'You tipped him off about the Minx?'

'I did – too true! And I gave him the dope about the slashings and the letter.'

This would redouble Stephens's eagerness; now, he would be chafing to capture Johnson. Remembering the Luger, Gently experienced a moment's uneasiness.

'Remind him when he calls in again, will you . . . ? If Johnson turns up he's to report and stay with him.'

So far the 'arduous routine' had brought in little of interest, though the fact that it was Sunday was in some degree responsible. The various Palette Group members, heartlessly indifferent to police requirements, had proceeded to disperse on their lawful weekend occasions. Up till lunchtime only three had been questioned – Aymas, Baxter and Seymour – and of these only Aymas had a really firm alibi; with another man, he'd been up tending a sick pedigree cow. Seymour, the shy smiler, was the most pregnable of the three. Stammering and blushing, he had admitted to being out till three with 'a woman'. He had got himself drunk and didn't remember where she had taken him – and so another bit of 'arduous routine' was in process.

'Did you get anything interesting out of Mallows this morning?'

Gently hedged. 'It's always worthwhile talking to Mallows. He recognized those capitals as being cut from *The Times* . . . and he's got some of the paper. He recognized it directly.'

'Did he now!' Hansom grounded his irons for a moment. 'Now that *is* interesting – very interesting indeed.'

'Naturally, I asked him if he had given any away.'

'And naturally he hadn't.'

Gently shrugged, and ate assiduously.

Why was he wanting to defend the shrewd-eyed artist? Because that, when you boiled it down, was what he was instinctively seeking to do. Right then he was holding back and trying to dampen Hansom's curiosity – throwing him titbits, as it were, to head him off from the main fact. But yet, while his hand had still lingered on the telephone, he had begun to comprehend, to see the way things had worked . . .

'Suppose he didn't give it away, then – suppose he sent that letter himself?'

'In that case, how did Mrs Johnson get the rest of the sheet?'

'He was lying, of course! He did give it to her.'

'Then he might equally well have given her the lot.'

'Yeah!' It was logical, but Hansom wasn't quite satisfied. His familiarity with Gently had perhaps taught him something. He sawed a long slice from his piece of steak, but sat looking at it for a while before raising it to his mouth. Then he chewed absent-mindedly, his fork still hovering.

'He was pally enough with Mrs Johnson, wasn't he? Used to take her out for lunch and that sort of thing?'

'So did a lot of others.'

'But they haven't got that paper! And she only had that piece, because I've sent Ephgrave to the flat to check. Now

184

if Johnson sent the letter he might have destroyed some remaining paper – that's possible. I agree, though, it could be more probable; but it's probable enough that she got half a sheet from Mallows – and that that's all she ever had: it's as probable as hell!'

'Then why did he admit to me that he had some?'

'You tell me, you've made a study of the bloke. All I can say is that he's making me curious . . . yeah, and wasn't he the last one to see her?'

'You've forgotten something important.' Still he was defending Mallows! Reluctantly, he was letting Hansom draw a decisive point from him. 'He couldn't have composed that letter because he didn't know about Johnson and Farrer. We didn't release it to the press, and Mallows wasn't there to be an eyewitness.'

'How do you know he wasn't there?'

'I had an appointment with him at eleven. He was waiting for me in his studio, and I found him working on a canvas.'

'Supposing Farrer rang up and told him?'

Gently with difficulty suppressed a smile. This was the first thing that people thought of; the easy, automatic, but quite transparent, explanation.

'I checked with Farrer, and Farrer didn't.'

'Huh! All the same, I keep being curious.'

'There could be another source for the paper, you know.'

'You bet – it's as common as muck, round here!'

Gently had succeeded nevertheless in heading Hansom away from Mallows, and the Chief Inspector was back to his old love by the time the rice pudding arrived. In a way, they had each of them made personal issues, Hansom with Johnson and Gently with Mallows. Though at first Gently had not regarded the artist as a 'hot' suspect, had he not been preparing himself for the moment when he would? Judas-like, he had let himself be attracted by Mallows . . . and now he felt compelled to keep the man to himself.

It was beginning to be a mystery where Johnson had disappeared to, whether or not he had shaved off that undisguisable moustache. The subject of an all-stations, the description of his car known, he had still completely eluded the attention of authority. Two reports had come in before the car details were available, and neither had stood up to a moment's scrutiny, but since the details had gone out there had been a uniform silence – Johnson's Minx appeared to have vanished, with the estate agent inside it.

Did he have some other bolt hole of which the police knew nothing? The Nearstead cottage was already under surveillance. On the chance, Hansom dispatched a detective to Johnson's office, with instructions to list all unsold property on the books.

After lunch Gently was able to fill in some details of his 'X' list. Allstanley had been traced: he was visiting some friends in the city. The balding teacher, who smoked a comfortable-looking cherrywood, drove voluntarily to Headquarters and was brought up to Hansom's office.

'Your people rang me up from my digs at Walford – asked me to come along to answer some questions.'

He had a quiet, pleasant voice and sensitive, retiring features, so that one wondered how he kept discipline in a crowded council school. After a while, however, one noticed a gentle authority. He thought before he spoke and made statements that were positive.

'No, I don't mind telling you where I was last night. I'm spending the weekend with the Todds, and we went to the Playhouse.'

'You slept at the Todds', did you?'

'They've put me up in their parlour. The kids being at home means they're without a spare bedroom.'

'So in fact you slept downstairs?'

'Yes, that's right.'

'You were the only one sleeping downstairs?'

'Of course – what's happened?'

On being told, he showed signs of dismay and wanted to hear the details. He looked solemn when he learnt the fate of his own precious exhibit.

'And I'd sold it, too – the first of my "wires" to go! But it's probably just as well. I would hardly have bashed my own "wire" . . .'

Having got him Gently was in no hurry to let Allstanley escape, but fired other questions at him, about the meeting and about Shirley Johnson. He was not so much interested in the answers as in the man's personality – there were several points about Allstanley which answered to Mallows's portrait.

'You were good friends with Mrs Johnson?'

'I'm not sure that I'd say that. I liked her well enough, but it didn't blind me to her faults.'

'Suppose I told you that she expressed herself as being fond of you, to Mr Mallows?'

An unbelieving stare, and then: 'He should know – he made the running with her.'

Gently hadn't bargained for that, but he couldn't let it pass: he could feel Hansom's dark eyes boring in from beside him.

'He took notice of her, did he?'

'You can put it like that if you want to.'

'Are you saying more than that?'

It was a challenge, and Allstanley shook his head.

But it continued to hang in the air, that unexpectedly dangerous response, and though Gently covered it up he couldn't entirely remove its impact. After Allstanley had gone Hansom tapped him on the shoulder:

'What do you say to her having blackmailed Mallows?'

It took Gently back to where Stephens had come in . . .

The reports, as they slowly arrived, bore a painful air of sameness. Few of the members could give foolproof alibis, though such as they had stood up to inquiry. Shoreby had spent the night on a houseboat, Wimbush was visiting his mother in Starmouth. Seymour's 'woman' was a well-known prostitute who occupied lodgings off Riverbank Road. The results of the searches were equally negative – no mutilated *Times*es or sheets of 'Leonardo da Vinci'; only Baxter, besides Mallows, was a subscriber to the former, and he produced his back numbers in a beautifully even pile.

It was ten minutes past three when the first excitement occurred, until when the day had seemed booked to end in a stalemate. Gently had just lit his pipe and was gazing down into the street – the sun had lately broken through, to evoke a higher incidence of strollers. Behind him he heard the phone buzz and Hansom picking it up.

'Chief Inspector Hansom . . . yes . . . that's right . . .

come again? He sold it? . . . well, the cheeky so-and-so! . . . yeah . . . I'll say! . . . yep, do that for me . . . thanks a lot . . . yeah . . . thanks.'

The receiver clunked down and Hansom made a crowing sound: 'So what do you know about that! The chummie goes and flogs the car!'

'You were talking about Johnson?'

'Yeah – that was Chelmsford on the wire. They've just spotted the Minx in a dealer's window – Johnson flogged it to him last night – made a tenner on the deal! Chelmsford are checking the buses and trains to see if they can pick up his trail for us.'

'Chelmsford, eh . . . ?'

'Yep – heading for the Smoke. He must have decided that the Minx was a bit too risky to stay with. But the craftiness of the boyo, flogging his car to another dealer! If Chelmsford hadn't been so spry, we might not have heard of it for days.'

'At what time did he sell the car?'

'It was yesterday evening, round about eight.'

'Did they ask if he's bought another?'

'Not from that establishment he didn't.'

Hansom picked up the phone again and Gently puffed some steady smoke rings. If Johnson had sold the car around eight, then how had he spent the rest of the time? To drive to Chelmsford would take two hours: he had been in possession of the Minx before noon. Thus there were six hours to be accounted for – a surprising delay, for a man on the run!

'Just a moment . . . let me have that phone!'

An Inspector Horrocks took the call at Chelmsford.

'In connection with Johnson . . . he's an ex-RAF pilot. Haven't you got a charter-flight firm operating near the town?'

They had, as he remembered, and Horrocks hastened to put him through to it; the connection all the same took an unconscionable time to get. Hansom, stricken by sudden visions of his prey escaping for good, sat cracking his knuckles in a ferment of impatience. At last:

'Wayland Charter Flights. Can we be of service?'

Gently carefully explained what he wanted to know.

'Oh, yes. That's the fellow who chartered our Proctor, X X-ray. He's got it for a week, doing cross-country flips . . .'

Five minutes later they knew all there was to know, which was that Johnson was probably clear of the country. He had taken off with full tanks at nine a.m. that morning, and in the still air conditions prevailing, must long since have touched down in France.

'He drove in here yesterday at half past two and asked if we had any light planes for charter. The Proctor had just come in and he took it up for a flip . . . he's a beautiful peelo, his three-point was a natural . . .

'He might have taken it away then – it had just had a one-twenty-hour inspection, but he preferred to wait and make his start this morning. We had it waiting on the tarmac and at ten to nine he took off for Lympne . . . yes, he paid for the charter in advance . . . he had a suitcase, and arrived in a taxi.'

A further call, to Lympne Airport, provided the necessary clincher. No Proctor from Wayland Charter Flights had been received that day. The only mystery that

remained concerned Johnson's curious lack of urgency –
why, in effect, had he delayed, when he might have made
his trip straight away?

'He hired a car and doubled back to do this slashing
lark!' – Hansom bit the end off a cheroot, spitting the
pieces into an ashtray. 'It's clear enough why he did it – he
wants to sell us on a crazy killer. So then we go and chase
our tails instead of chasing chummie Johnson.'

It was a theory that fitted and left no visible gaps.
Johnson, possessed of means and motive, could easily
arrange the opportunity. After he had chartered the plane,
no doubt, he had bought a *Times* and concocted the letter.
Then, having sold the too-risky Minx, he had hired a car
and returned to the city . . . It was all of a piece, including
the knowledge shown in the letter. There only remained
that perpetual query – was Johnson really so fiendishly
clever?

'Where do you suppose he got the other knife?'

'What was to stop him from buying one in Chelmsford?'

Gently shrugged. 'They're an obsolete pattern, so he
couldn't have chanced buying one down there. It was the
nub of the plot, that other knife, and he must have had it
before he did the letter. Thus he must have had it before he
skipped, or why did he take the piece of paper with him?'

'He's a bright lad, you can't get away from it.'

'He's a genius – or somebody is.'

The tracing of the knife was already in hand but was
being frustrated, like other inquiry, by the fact that it was
Sunday. The owner of the shop which carried a stock of
the knives had been reported as having taken his family on
a picnic.

Gently rang through to the Yard, and by luck caught Pagram. 'I want a watch at all airports, just in case he lands somewhere. And his description to Interpol, with details of the flight . . .

'And by the way – congratulations on getting Peachfield tied up.'

Hansom smoked three cheroots in rapid succession, his expression becoming more embittered the more he brooded over Johnson's escape. He glared tigerishly through the smoke at the now brilliant afternoon, and snapped at the constable who brought them up a tray of coffee. He was, Gently could feel, blaming the Yard man for all this – wouldn't a policeman with correct principles have arrested Johnson on Friday night? There was the clearest of cases against him, a case to rejoice the public prosecutor, and the passage of time had only strengthened it further . . .

'Aren't you going to tell your playmate that he's wasting his time?'

Gently grinned distantly at his disgruntled colleague. On the face of it, perhaps . . . but the face of it was deceptive! It had been so on Friday night, and it was no less so on Sunday. And it was on Mallows, not Johnson, that Gently's mind ceaselessly dwelt, remembering, checking and persistently setting in balance. The time was surely coming when they must try their strengths together, and as an experienced antagonist, he was weighing up his opponent. In the academician he could recognize a champion among mental fencers.

'This time you're going to charge him, I suppose?'

From the depths of his gloom Hansom dredged the sarcasm.

'I want to talk to him – badly. He's got the answer to a vital question.'

'You talked to him before – and now he's in France!'

What was the use of taking offence? One was obliged to sympathize with Hansom. At his best he was a jealous and surly kind of man. Twice before, once unofficially, Gently had taken a case away from him, and now, without rhyme or reason, he had let Hansom's 'chummie' slide through his fingers . . .

'Don't take it to heart . . . we'll get him in the end.' To Stephens he had used almost the selfsame words.

'I can see us doing that now he's got across the Channel! Don't forget he isn't a rabbit – he's the original cobber from Colditz.'

'All the same, he'll be up against it. He doesn't have professional contacts.'

They were interrupted by the inexorable phone, bringing, this time, a report on Lavery. It was negative; but before Hansom could vent his disgust the instrument clicked and began buzzing again. Gently saw a change come over Hansom's face. From antagonism it slid into blank perplexity. After a number of surprised-sounding monosyllables he concluded:

'Yeah – we'll have them sent straight away up!'

A minute later, during which time Hansom had said nothing, a detective constable entered carrying an official envelope. He had the complacent expression which Dutt sometimes wore, the expression of a man who had pulled off something good.

'Shake them out on the desk.' Hansom sounded suspicious, and his eye all the while rested pointedly on

Gently. The man opened the envelope and slid the contents out cautiously: they comprised one mutilated *Times* – and a third steel paper knife!

'Tell the Superintendent where you found them!'

Now there could be no doubting it. Hansom's tone, like his look, was eloquent of what he was thinking.

'At Mr Mallows's, sir – and we very nearly missed them. They were hidden under the matting outside his front porch.'

If Hansom was unconvinced that Gently hadn't foreseen this find there were adequate reasons for it in the latter's sparse reactions. Though Gently, on occasion, had been known to show emotion, the present did not seem to be one of those times.

'Get your print man on to them.' His steady blankness was impervious – after a moment's inspection of the exhibits, he seemed to have exhausted his interest. Still poker-faced, he knocked out his pipe and refilled it, and then quietly sat down at the side of the desk. Hansom, looking uncertain, waved a hand to the detective constable, then he too resumed his seat at the desk.

'Well . . . that certainly gives the thing a different look!'

'Hmm.' Gently's grunt was an archetype of neutrality.

'If I'd guessed about that' – Hansom stared hard across the desk – 'I wouldn't have been too worried about Johnson, either . . .'

The cue was plainly Gently's, but just as plainly, he wasn't taking it, and instead his eyes had lapsed into that distant, absent expression. Those like Dutt who knew him well could have suggested what this meant, but to Hansom it merely suggested that Gently wasn't quite with him.

'Let's see where it gets us.' Hansom grew tired of waiting. If Gently wouldn't play, he was going to press on without him. 'Mallows was stuck on Mrs Johnson, and he was the last person to see her alive. Her picture was painted on a special paper and Mallows has got some of that special paper. The letter was also on that paper, and it referred to another knife: and the knife, plus a mutilated *Times*, is found concealed at Mallows's house.

'So what is a policeman going to think when he's being a common, ornery policeman? He's going to think that we should pull in Mallows and have a cosy, comfortable chat with him!'

Gently blew him a puff of smoke by way of reward for this performance. 'Don't ever rush a fence like Mallows . . . you're liable to wind up in the ditch.'

'Does that paper and knife look like we're rushing something?'

'At least we can wait to check them for prints. And it might be wise to compare the *Times* with the letter, just in case someone has tried to work a ringer.'

'And who in the blue blazes would do that?'

'I don't know . . . think it over for yourself. But in either case we'll need to check the prints, to find if Mallows's are actually on *The Times*.'

'They won't be. Chummie doesn't leave his prints.'

'Then surely you can see the implication? Mallows would hardly have been so careful as to handle the paper with gloves – nor would anyone else, except for a very special purpose.'

'You mean' – Hansom struggled to grasp this knotty point – 'unless chummie was expecting us to find the paper?'

'Just so – in the normal way, you'd expect the paper to be destroyed. It would be much easier to do that than to cut out small capitals while wearing gloves.'

'Yeah!' Hansom paused to let the idea sink in. But only a moment or so was necessary to deduce the grateful consequence:

'So like that, Johnson may have planted it!'

'I don't see why not.'

'Sneaked in after he did the job, and popped the evidence under the boyo's doormat! Because he knew darned well that there'd be a search – there'd have to be, after Farrer showed us the letter; and if he knew where his missus had got the gash paper – bingo! Mallows was sitting right in the target area.'

Gently blew some more smoke at this promising pupil. 'We can assume, I dare say, that Johnson knew about his wife and Mallows . . .'

'Hell yes! It stands out. There's revenge in this too – he may have plotted it from the beginning to throw suspicion on Mallows. Or maybe just to drag him in, to roll his character in the mud: and this is the crafty way he's done it – killing a couple of birds at once.'

'He's a bright lad, as you were saying.'

'Yeah – only not so bright as he thinks!'

In common with the group members, Mallows had had his prints taken, so there was the briefest of delays in checking the fresh evidence. As Gently had surmised, the artist's prints were not on the *Times*; it showed only the detective constable's and a pair of others, not on record. A comparison with the letter disposed of the other point – this was the veritable *Times* which had supplied the

196

characters. The knife, needless to say, was bright and unsmirched, and identical in pattern with its two predecessors.

They had tea, like lunch, sitting at Hansom's special table, and the local man was too absorbed to notice Gently's continued abstraction. He was busy devising plans for the further and decisive trapping of Johnson, and was now triumphant, now subdued, according to the aspect that came uppermost.

'We'll get Chelmsford to identify those spare sets of prints – they're bound to find them at one of the newsagents. Then an identity parade, as soon as we lay hold of Johnson . . . it's the devil, that chummie being able to fly!

'And then there's the knives. Of course, you're right about them being bought here. The whole thing was planned, not done on the spur of the moment. Johnson hated the Palette Group because his wife ran around with it, he's got the natural motive for wanting to slash those pictures . . .

'So we'll get on to the supplier, who probably recognized Johnson anyway . . . if not, it's only a question of another identity parade. There's this to be said for that chummie, he isn't difficult to pick out – once seen, never forgotten, not unless he's lost his moustache . . .

'Where do you reckon he headed for – was it Orly, or somewhere quieter?'

While they were eating another report was brought in, but now Hansom had no use for these tedious messages. The events of the day, though occasionally teasing, had all finally supported his dogged contention. He could see only

Johnson, fenced in by every circumstance. Whatever line you chose took you straight to the estate agent. Like a spider he was sitting in the middle of a web of facts, and though at times they spiralled round him, their connection was never severed.

It was Johnson who was Hansom's chummie – however far he meant to roam!

'A message from Inspector Stephens, sir . . .'

Hansom deafened his ears to this fresh invasion of privacy. At the moment there was only one message he wanted to hear about, and that must come via the Yard, from the Quai des Orfèvres. By a stretch of imagination he could picture the desired event, he could see two sombre figures waiting to greet the taxiing Proctor . . . 'M. Johnson, I believe? You must accompany us, monsieur' – followed by a call from the nearest phone box, and a quick relaying of the news . . .

Irritably, he noticed that Gently was speaking to him:

'We'll take your car, then, and get on the road . . .'

'Take my car where?'

'Why! After Stephens, naturally.'

'What the blazes for – hasn't he got a car of his own?'

He was aware that Gently was looking at him oddly, and then of the slow smile that spread over the Superintendent's face.

'Didn't you hear the message he sent? Miss Butters has vamoosed in her sister's Jaguar, and Stephens is busy tailing her, in a westerly direction . . .'

'Miss Butters . . . *on her own*?'

'Yes, driving fairly fast. And I don't think she's gone after a breath of fresh air . . .'

They were mobile in minutes, with Hansom taking the wheel; Gently barely had time to retrieve his pipe from the office. Two of the minutes, however, had been judiciously spent: they were occupied in the signing out of a police-issue Webley.

CHAPTER TWELVE

B Y THE TIME they had got clear of the city streets, Gently was beginning to feel sorry that he had let Hansom drive. The Chief Inspector, with all due allowance for his eagerness, was not a model of the correct and approved police driver. His deficiencies were the more apparent because they were meeting a flow of traffic. The spasmodic efflux of Saturday had become the steady influx of Sunday. It might have been worse, it was true: they were on the Fosterham Road; towards Starmouth, the traffic would now be packed in nose to tail. But there was plenty enough here to produce some breathtaking moments, and what was worse to suggest that such were commonplaces of Hansom's style.

Over his knees Gently had spread the three-inch map from the car's pocket, and on this, with pencilled crosses, he was plotting their progress. They were in constant radio contact with the pursuing Stephens, who was conscientious in reporting every location he passed.

'Hallo car ex–two . . . we've just come to a village . . . get you the name if I can . . . yes . . . Saxham King's Head!'

On a more southerly route they were catching up with the other two, whose progress was governed by the whims of Miss Butters. She was making straight across country with all the confidence of local knowledge, never hesitating to use a side road where its line was the most direct.

'Hallo car ex-two . . . she's just stopped for petrol . . . I had to go past her . . . don't think she noticed . . . am waiting in side road, Braningham one mile.'

'Hallo car ex-seven . . . don't follow her so closely!'

'Hallo car ex-two . . . message understood.'

Gently held up the map so that Hansom could glance at it, the pencilled crosses now strung out in purposeful direction. 'Does it suggest anything to you?'

'Yeah – she's heading for Fosterham. They've got a flying club there, but surely he wouldn't have the nerve . . .'

'I'll call back to HQ.' Gently flicked the switch across. To him too it seemed unlikely that Johnson would use an operational airfield. But, for all the estate agent knew, his latest ploy was undetected, and he might be unwarily sitting in the club house at Fosterham.

'Car ex-two calling ex-ex-ex . . . I'd like you to get in touch with the County at Fosterham. Johnson may be at the flying club . . . tell them to send a couple of men. And remind them that he's armed . . . repeat that: armed!'

'Ex-ex-ex replying to car ex-two . . . message received and understood, and I have one for you . . . Lady Stradsett reports the loss of a grey Jaguar convertible, believed to have been taken from Lordham Grange at around seventeen-thirty hours . . . do you want any independent action on this?'

'Hallo ex-ex-ex . . . no independent action.'

The Wolseley drummed along at an unsteady sixty, with Hansom juggling rhapsodically with his brakes and throttle. It was in fact a good lick for that contorted country road, on which the stream of homing traffic was unceasing though irregular. On either side there was country which was typical of upland Northshire. It proceeded in gentle undulations with shaggy hedges and wistful trees. It had the muted and subdued charm of an unlistened-to sonata which, some day, one suddenly noticed had made a haunting and fixed impression. It was difficult to pin it down to any single feature. The villages, for example, had little truck with the picturesque. Like the landscape they were stern, but with an unaffected nobility, and one sensed a majestic strength which lay beneath the austere surface.

Farther on the contours were higher but the astringent flavour remained; only here one could see more into it, more deeply probe the secret amalgam. There were glimpses of square flint towers, of ranked plantations, like armies marching; of farmhouses glowing in rusty brick, and monstrous barns with huge, peaked roofs. And the fields were seen quilted with colour, the yellow of mustard, the green of beet; and everywhere, dashed with poppies, the tawny wheat and paler acres of barley.

Even from a Hansom-driven Wolseley one was compelled to observe and admire, and Gently, to whom the road was fresh, made a mental note to return in his Riley . . .

'Car ex-seven calling car ex-two . . . passing through a small town . . . it's Fosterham, I think.'

Gently jabbed to transmit: 'Hallo ex-seven . . . watch carefully here . . . she may turn off to the flying field.'

But half a minute later Stephens came through again:

'We're out at the other side . . . still driving in the same direction . . .'

So Fosterham was out. It wasn't as simple as that. The wary ex-RAF pilot was doing nothing that might betray himself . . .

'Any more suggestions?' Gently tilted the map again, having just scrawled a cross on the far side of Fosterham. They too were approaching the town and would soon be hard on Stephens's tail; there could not now be more than a few miles separating them.

'If it was a question of boats, I'd say she was heading for the coast . . . as it is . . .' Hansom frowned, giving a flickering look at the map. 'The trouble is there's two . . . no, three . . . old air-force dromes out that way, and they're all in roughish country – just left to rot there, after the war.'

'They sound a better prospect.'

'Yeah . . . but it may not be so easy. It's heathy country, you can see for miles – and chummie'll have that angle covered.'

It went without saying. Johnson didn't miss his tricks. If there was an advantage to be gained he could be relied upon to take it. Gently brooded for a few moments over the advisability of calling on help, but under the circumstances there seemed little open to them that would give them a better chance. In the first place, they didn't yet know for certain where they were going . . .

'Car ex-seven calling car ex-two . . . we're turning off south about five miles from Fosterham. Signpost says By-road and there's a straw stack beside it . . . half a dozen tar barrels parked on the verge.'

Gently referred to the map, but they were in a country of by-roads; narrow parallels, some dotted, straying out into blank spaces.

'Calling car ex-seven . . . drop back as far as you can . . . you're going into open country, you'll be able to see her well ahead.'

Then they were in Fosterham, making the townspeople stare – Hansom wasn't in a mood to defer to country towns. Gently received a snapshot impression of a street of plastered house fronts, a sleepy market square and a hovering flint tower. A pleasant place, probably – but the Wolseley whisked him past it. Beyond it, almost directly, they entered a sparser-looking tract of country.

Here the trees which had graced every hedgerow were become few and mean in appearance, and the fields, snowed with chalk-backed flints, supported thin and starve-acre crops. The hedges likewise had shrunk to mere scrub, soon to be choked and replaced by bracken; one saw far distances of brackened slopes scarred by gravel and by droves of sand.

'Now you can see what I mean.' Hansom made an embracing motion with his hand. 'It goes on like this for miles, and farther down it's a battle area. But I'd say she was making for Rawton, that's what it sounds like, turning down there.'

'Is there anything else in that direction?'

'Yeah . . . she might find a way to Morsingdon.'

They identified the turning by Stephens's description and found themselves on a road with a surface that made Hansom swear. It had patently been neglected for a number of years – in all probability, since the end of the war. A rusted service sign confirmed this conjecture. Farther on, they passed a dump of disintegrating barbed wire. On both sides of the road stretched the god-forgotten heathland, relieved only at long intervals by ragged and wind-sculptured firs.

'Car ex-seven calling car ex-two . . . she's going very slowly . . . not sure of the way. There's practically no road . . . just a track of broken concrete . . . I've stopped behind a pill box . . . we'll have to let her get ahead . . .'

'Calling car ex-seven . . . do we just keep straight on?'

'Calling car ex-two . . . slow down where you see a gun emplacement.'

Hansom was still bumping along at a stubborn forty-five, though the Wolseley was taking a hammering from potholes and sunken surfaces. Now, however, the metalled surface petered out entirely, giving way to a stony track which looked as aboriginal as the heath. In front of them it stretched away into a hollow or valley where the bracken-covered slopes shouldered closely to each other; it was deep enough to take a shadow from the westering sun, and was guarded by two tattered firs standing one to either side.

As they approached it they saw evident signs of a former occupation. A picket hut stood ruinous to one side of the track. Beside it lay a fallen gate and a w.d. property notice and, a little higher up, the gun emplacement referred to by Stephens.

'They must have loved being stationed here . . . !' Hansom clashed to a lower gear. The Wolseley slithered and yawed a little as it scrambled over some crumbling concrete. Almost immediately they were turning a corner, and then the need for caution was plain: they were coming out on the brow of a slope, from which they must be visible for at least a mile. Hansom jammed on the brakes abruptly.

'If he was anywhere near her, she would have seen him . . .'

Gently nodded, puckering his eyes as he searched the sweep of country before them. The heath here was very level and without a lot of cover, though leftwards, to the south, it slowly rose into a shallow ridge. Down the track, perhaps a quarter of a mile away, one could make out a pair of battered pill boxes.

He flicked the radio to transmit:

'Calling car ex-seven . . . report your movements.'

After a minute, when there was no reply, he repeated the call with greater urgency.

Still there was no response from Stephens. Hansom met Gently's eye as he tried again.

'What do you make of that . . . would he have gone off on a recce?'

'I don't know. But I warned him to keep clear of trouble . . .'

It was at that instant that they heard the sound of a shot, coming distant but distinct from behind the southerly slope. A second later it was repeated by a second and a third, each producing a ringing echo from the stony little hollow.

'Brother . . . let's go!' Hansom jerked in the clutch. The Wolseley went bumbling forward over the outrageous concrete track. Foot down, Hansom lashed the tortured vehicle into the fifties, making it bound and bucket like a goaded stallion. The track bore to the left through an area of scrubby bushes, but some distance beyond the pill boxes it apparently vanished into the naked heath. Swearing viciously, Hansom blazed on along the line it had been taking, the sheer power of his anger seeming to keep the car going.

'Over there – keep left!'

The track was coming to light again. Making a sudden turn to the left, it dived into an unexpected grove of firs. A pearl-grey Jaguar leapt into sight and Hansom dragged on the wheel like a madman; the Wolseley twisted from stem to stern, wiped past a tree, then straightened again. And then they were out on the southern side of the ridge, with the abandoned airfield stretching ahead of them: and there, developing at a speed which defied interference, was the drama which Stephens's silence had portended.

Johnson's Proctor had commenced its take-off from the adjacent end of a runway – a runway which, one could see, was badly damaged by cracks and sinkings. Its tail was already rising, its engine rolling at full throttle, it had the bit between its teeth and it was irresistibly tearing forwards. Irresistibly – except for one thing. The other Wolseley was racing towards it. Stephens must have driven down the runway ahead of it, and now, circling round, was dead in its path.

Something caught in Gently's throat as he took in the spectacle, for what must happen was well-nigh inevitable. It was impossible to apply the brakes to the Proctor, and the Wolseley showed no intention of budging.

'The prop – the engine – they'll sheer him in halves—!' He watched it in the grip of a ghastly compulsion; the searing experience of those few seconds seemed to suspend and to expand into several hours. But at the moment of impact, the unforeseen happened. The Proctor flew up like a great catherine wheel. Digging its nose into the ground, it spun crashingly over and over, hurling fragments in all directions across the heath-covered soil. And Stephens, he rumbled on up the runway unharmed, his tyres a-shriek as he stamped on his brakes. He brought the Wolseley X-7 to a jerking halt: he didn't seem even to have scratched her paintwork.

Seeing that Stephens was unharmed, Hansom drove on towards the aircraft, which had finally come to rest lying flat on its belly. One wing was wrenched off and the other was badly damaged, while the propeller had been twisted into savage, unnatural shapes. The undercarriage, sheered away, had flown to various parts of the compass, and the port side of the tail assembly hung in raw-looking ribbons. Of the occupants, Miss Butters was lying slumped against the control panel, while Johnson was feebly trying to force back the perspex hood.

In emergencies of this kind, Hansom was a good man to have around. He wasted no time in words or panicky actions. He was out of the Wolseley almost before it had stopped, and leaping up on the wing root, had begun to work on the jammed hood.

'Get us out of this, cocker . . . we're swimming in petrol . . . !'

It was true, the stuff was pouring from a fractured pipe in the wing root. In addition the engine was simmering, sounding like a sinister boiler, giving every now and then little popping and cracking noises.

'This bastard thing's twisted . . . to hell, it's twisted!'

'Is there an axe in the car?'

'Yeah – get it, for Christ's sake!'

Gently dropped down from the wing and ran to the boot of the Wolseley. He found a fireman's axe and a jemmy in the tool kit it contained.

Stephens, meanwhile, came bumping up in the second Wolseley, and trembling and pale added his efforts to theirs.

'He . . . he did that deliberately . . .'

'Turned off, you mean?'

'Yes . . . oh God . . . we've got to get them out of there!'

'What about those shots?'

'He was shooting at my tyres . . . let me have something . . . let me! . . . we've got to get them out!'

He seized the jemmy from Gently's hand and began furiously levering with it, Hansom at the same time delivering crashing blows with the axe. Johnson had sunk down into his seat and appeared to have lost consciousness. Anne Butters didn't stir from her prone position.

At last the hood was freed and by brute force torn off, and the admission of fresh air seemed to revive Johnson a little.

'Jesus . . . take it easy! My leg's buggered up . . .' Trying to move, he went suddenly white, then his head dropped forward again.

Gently and Stephens got him out – it was not an easy business then; his fractured leg, sticky with blood, had become entangled with the controls. He was fortunate perhaps to remain unconscious during the process, and he continued in that state while they carried him behind the cars. Hansom took care of Anne Butters on his own. Apart from being out, she showed no sign of any injury. For fear of internal injury he was nevertheless cautious, and handled her with a gentleness that one would not have suspected of him.

'I'll strap up the boyo's leg . . . I'm a first-aid wizard.'

'First we must get them away from here – and likewise the cars.'

'We didn't ought to shift them . . .'

'Suppose that wreck goes up!'

'Yeah, I see what you mean . . . right. We'll use that chunk of wing for a stretcher.'

At a safer distance of seventy yards they parked the two Wolseleys to make a screen, and behind it, assisted by a drooping Stephens, Hansom strapped and bandaged Johnson's leg. Before commencing he gave the estate agent a jab from a morphia ampoule, taking care to find the label and to tie it to his patient. It was really a revelation to watch the Chief Inspector at work – he was displaying a side of his surly nature which had rarely come uppermost.

'That'll fix you, sonny, till we can get you to a hospital.'

Johnson managed to grin at him from under his immense moustache.

'But Anne . . . what about . . . ?' His eyes flickered glazedly to the limp figure.

'Don't worry about her. She was only knocked out cold.'

Just then, when they had given up expecting it to happen; a sudden woof of flame sprang up from the wreckage; in moments it had turned into a roaring, wolfish pillar, and a great jet of black smoke puffed into the sky above it. There was nothing they could do – their car extinguishers were futile. One might as well have tackled it with a glass of water. Stephens, back in his car, was trying to raise Fosterham, their own control being now out of range.

Miss Butters stirred and her eyes fell open, vacantly; then, at the snarling sound of the flames, they jumped wide in fear. Johnson's lids were closed and he was murmuring thickly to himself:

'. . . Christ . . . Christ . . . I wasn't meant to die that way . . .'

Stephens eventually contacted the control at Lynton, but they phoned through to Fosterham as being the nearest to Rawton Aerodrome. Some half an hour later quite a cavalcade appeared, its component vehicles rocking and pitching as they negotiated the frightful surface. First came two mounted police, who had been acting as pathfinders, and now fanned out impatiently as they came to the scene of the crash. They were followed by a police car and a bobbing white ambulance, and finally by an RAF fire tender, hastily summoned from the nearest camp.

The latter drove across to the wreck and began to engulf it in white foam, though there was little now left of it except the engine and bearers. From the ambulance jumped down a pair of overalled attendants. They carried a rolled-up stretcher which they silently unbuckled.

'Inspector Vincent, County Police . . . pleased to make your acquaintance, sir.'

All of a sudden the place seemed to be alive with awkward policemen. They had really nothing to do except to stand about watching – only the ambulancemen and the fire tender had jobs to keep them busy.

Anne Butters, though pale and shaken, seemed little the worse for her experience. She drank coffee from somebody's flask but didn't stray far from Johnson's side.

'He'll be all right . . . his leg is all right . . . ?'

She was putting a brave, a correct 'county' face on it; one could almost imagine that this was a hunting mishap, and that the Master would shortly ride up to make inquiries. With Gently she would have nothing whatever to do. She ignored him with the ferocious disdain of 'county' protocol. Hansom, too, was cold-shouldered, though oddly enough, not Stephens; in reality she was near a breakdown, and would have burst into tears if they had turned their backs.

'That's a nasty bump on your forehead, miss . . .'

'It's all right, I tell you! They've put some stuff on it.'

'Well, we'll give you a run over when we get you to the hospital . . .'

'No, I'm all right! It's Derek . . . it's Derek . . .'

Here she had to break off and bite her lips together, but immediately she turned fiercely on the hovering Stephens:

'Now, I suppose, they're going to charge Derek with something or other!'

Stephens blushed and mumbled confusedly, but she didn't wait to hear his reply.

Gently rapidly explained the situation to Vincent; he didn't want to be delayed when the ambulance set off. In the name of mercy he had refrained from stopping Hansom using the morphia, but there were crucial questions of which he wanted the answers from Johnson. He grabbed one of the attendants.

'They're not to dope him before I've talked to him . . . you've seen that label – he shouldn't need any more for a bit.'

The attendant shrugged. 'I can't promise you anything, sir. You'll have to come to the hospital and talk to them there.'

This time he drove himself, in Stephens's Wolseley. Hansom, who hadn't been saying much, followed erratically in their rear. Stephens was also rather quiet, but there was nothing surprising in that: his exploit in stopping Johnson must have given him plenty to think about.

'That was a damn silly thing to do . . . !'

'Yes, sir.' Stephens drooped his head. Gently had no need to specify the subject of his remark.

'There'll be times enough to play the hero without your cooking any up – suppose the fellow *had* got away, how far do you think he could have gone?'

'Well, sir, considering his known abilities—'

'Considering my foot! He might have got to the Continent, or perhaps to Eire. He's without professional contacts, and he was tagging a woman along with him – and we could have followed him with radar – maybe chivvied him down with fighters.

'Yet you go and risk your neck in a bit of Dick Barton foolery – risked the life of the girl, too, not to mention the ratepayers' property!'

'I didn't mean to smash him, sir.'

'What the devil else could you have done?'

'I just wanted to block his take-off . . . then . . . well, it all happened so fast.'

'Huh!' Gently's grunt was in the Hansom tradition, but he could easily visualize what had taken place. Petrified by the oncoming plane, Stephens had simply hung on and prayed: his reflexes had been paralysed by the speed of what had happened. With his foot hard down he had rushed fascinated towards disaster . . .

'You're lucky that Johnson didn't lose his head, too.'

'Yes, sir, I realize that. I think he was expecting me to pull out.'

'And those shots were at your tyres?'

'Yes, sir. They weren't at me. He must have guessed what I intended to do, and tried to put my car out of action.'

From the way his young colleague spoke it was apparent that Johnson had won an admirer. The estate agent was no longer a middle-aged curio, a fossilized relic of some pre-atomic war. He had displayed his 'known abilities' in a way that was unforgettable, and Stephens, who had found himself wanting, was a little guiltily impressed.

'Anyway, it took guts . . .' Gently purposely left that vague; but he noticed that Stephens tilted his chin up and stole a glance towards his senior.

'Car ex-two calling car ex-seven . . .'

In his driving mirror he could see Hansom, the microphone in his hand.

'What do you know about Johnson . . . are we going to make the pinch?'

Coming from Hansom, this surely had to be admiration too!

'Car ex-seven calling car ex-two . . . considering all the circumstances, what do you recommend?'

'Calling car ex-seven . . . you'd better pinch him, I suppose, though if the evidence wasn't so one-track . . . damnation, you've *got* to pinch him!'

Even Hansom had his moments of intuition, it seemed, when the hard grain of logic met the steel edge of conviction. They were few and they were tardy, but he was not completely without them: against his settled inclination, he occasionally had a hunch . . .

'Calling car ex-seven . . . he pulled that kite over deliberately. I had a look at the runway – it's got a good surface just there.'

'Calling car ex-two . . . he'd be dead if he hadn't.'

'Calling car ex-seven . . . yeah, I see your point.'

Gently turned his head, concealing his smile from Stephens. The two of them were ganging up in their desire to whitewash Johnson! And in both cases it seemed to be his cool head that impressed them, though logically it was a factor which should stand in his disfavour. What was the process by which the logical suddenly collapsed and committed suicide – what was the mechanism of secret judgement which could destroy the pretensions of thought?

He paused, seeming once again on the threshold of revelation, for wasn't it thus that he always proceeded, checking logic by that inner judgement? It was the product, he suddenly saw, of his continuous stream of observation, a perpetual record of fact too huge and complete to be fully conscious. And so, detached from that stream, he had found his desk-work intolerable, he had been set to make bricks with only the vestiges of straw. For he was not a thinking man, but an artist pursuing a truth: in a way Mallows had been right. Gently was a sham as a policeman.

'Car ex-seven calling car ex-two . . .'

What had he been going to say to Hansom? It had gone clean out of his head . . .

They were in Fosterham by nine, travelling this time less sensationally. The ambulance clanged them through the town and into the yard of the red-brick hospital. Gently

215

was out of the Wolseley directly, pushing through the swing doors labelled RECEPTION. Beyond them he found an aseptic-looking hall in which were mingled the smells of ether and floor polish.

'Superintendent Gently, CID . . . I'd like to speak to the doctor in charge of Casualties.'

'The doctor is busy just now, I'm afraid. If you'll wait in the office I'll tell him you're here.'

She was a hard-eyed ward sister who quizzed Gently with disapproval; she went, nevertheless, to execute the errand. Gently stood in the doorway of the office and watched the attendants unload Johnson – he was conscious, though drowsy, and tried to wink as he was carried past. Anne Butters had been crying, but was not crying now. She walked with one hand on the stretcher, very erect, her chin in the air.

As they approached the door to Casualties they met the doctor coming out – a tall, youngish-looking man, who gave an exclamation of surprise.

'Anne! Well, I'm blowed! What on earth are you doing here?'

Quickly she tugged on his arm, jerking her head towards Gently. It was all over in a moment: with a significant nod, he hustled them through. Gently, racing to push in after them, found his passage barred by the ward sister.

'I'm sorry, Superintendent, but you can't come in here.'

'It's extremely important that I speak to the doctor!'

'He knows you are here and he will see you in a minute. As usual on Sundays, we are having a busy time.'

Short of brushing her aside physically, there was nothing that he could do about it. He stood glaring impotently at the door which even policemen couldn't open. In a couple of minutes the doctor came out again, but those minutes had done the damage; his gaunt young face was earnestly determined, and he put finality into his tone:

'There is very little use in your waiting, Superintendent. I cannot permit the patient Johnson to be seen again today.'

'Are his injuries so serious?'

'That we'll know when we've seen the X-ray. I assure you there's no point in your waiting any longer.'

'And that applies to Miss Butters?'

'She is suffering from delayed shock.'

'Couldn't it be delayed a little longer?'

'I will not take that suggestion seriously . . .'

Looking indignant, the doctor turned to go back into Casualties, but he was prevented by a hand placed firmly on his arm.

'Into the office, my lad! This isn't as simple as you seem to think. There's a little more hangs to it than your playing the Sir Galahad . . .'

Colouring, the doctor allowed himself to be conducted into the office. Gently closed the glass-panelled door, and finding no bolt, set his shoulder against it.

'Now! This is a case of murder, if you're slow at cottoning on.'

'I am perfectly aware of that—'

'Good. I'll try to enlighten you a bit further.

'You realize what has happened when a man commits homicide? In the first place, to do it, he's crossed the border of normality. Then, having done it, he's in arms against society – all other criminals have their friends, but the murderer stands alone.

217

'He's in arms against society! There's nothing still remaining sacred. He will kill again, or destroy, doing whatever seems to give him an advantage. And the murderer we are dealing with has begun his career of violence – with him, the murder was a point of departure, not a culminating act.

'He's more than the average killer – he's a man in the throes of a primary breakdown; still able to counterfeit normality, but in a state of moral collapse. And if my surmise is correct then Johnson can help me to identify him – tonight, in all probability, before he has a chance to do more damage.

'So now you know where you stand. I'm putting the responsibility on you. Either you let me talk to Johnson, or what may happen will rest on your shoulders.'

The doctor, listening sullenly at first, became by degrees more thoughtful; then he gave Gently a curious, half wondering look.

'How long will it take?'

'At the outside, five minutes.'

'Come on then. We thought you were going to shove handcuffs on the bloke.'

Johnson was lying on a couch and he still appeared drowsy, but he was mumbling something to Anne Butters, who sat holding his hand. Seeing Gently with the doctor she rose angrily to her feet, but the latter made her a sign and then whispered:

'It's all right!'

Unwillingly she stood back and permitted Gently to take the chair. Johnson turned his head slightly, his eyes questioning Gently.

'How are you feeling now, Johnson?'

'Doped . . . and damned glad of it! Couldn't you wait a bit, cocker . . . let them set this bastard?'

'There's some questions I have to ask you.'

'Whacko! . . . I knew it . . .'

'I want to know what you did after you sold your car last night.'

Johnson frowned, though whether from pain it wasn't easy to decide. There were deep creases about his eyes and a square set to his mouth.

'What do you want to know . . . about that?'

'Everything. All you can remember.'

'I tried to get Anne on the phone . . . twice . . . wanted to tell her where to find me.'

'Did you get through to her?'

'No . . . this morning . . . when they went to church . . . reckoned that would be the time.'

'What else did you do?'

'I can't remember . . . went to the flicks.'

'Where was that?'

'Damn! High Street . . . Cary Grant in a horse opera.'

'And after that?'

'I went to bed.'

'Where? Where did you spend the night?'

'What does it matter? I don't know! . . . Bed and brekker in Church Street . . .'

'What was the name of the people?'

'Blast it, cocker . . . have a heart! Got a knocker like a horseshoe . . . remember that, it's why I went there . . .'

He was frowning more and more, and the doctor shook his head at Gently. Anne Butters, as though taking a cue, began decorously to weep. Gently shrugged and rose to his feet:

'I'd like to use your phone, if I may . . .'

'You'll find one in the office – now, I must really get him to Radiology.'

Gently's first call was to Headquarters where he made an unexpected connection – Superintendent Walker, who had heard news of Johnson's capture. The city police chief had driven in from his house on the outskirts, and was now waiting impatiently to learn the sensational details.

'Have you pinned the charge on him?'

'No – not yet! There's one or two more things which need tying up. I'll be back in about an hour and we'll talk it over then . . . in the meantime, will you post a man outside Mallows's house?'

'Mallows! Has he got something to do with this?'

'I think he can help us . . .' Gently made a face. 'I'll want him for questioning as soon as I get back. But don't waste any time about putting a man on him.'

His second call was to Chelmsford, to Inspector Horrocks, to whom he gave the details he had learnt from Johnson.

'It's urgent to have them checked with the least possible delay. Ring me back at City Headquarters – I'll be available all night.'

All night . . . or as long as it took Mallows to crack. He went in search of Stephens and Hansom, and took them off for a cup of coffee.

CHAPTER THIRTEEN

I**T WAS CURIOUS** how, with no direct information available, everybody had a sense of approaching climax; even the remote subordinates in distant corners of HQ who seemed linked together by some psychic grapevine. In part it was perhaps an intelligent reading of events. Though Johnson had been found, he had not been proceeded against. Nor had Gently taken himself off to his hotel by the Castle, and as late at night as this he was prepared to summons Mallows. Unless he was hot on a scent, wouldn't the morning have done as well? And would Walker, who liked his eight hours, be preparing for a nocturnal session?

This odd feeling of tension had extended itself to the press men, half a dozen of whom Gently found playing rummy in the waiting room. There was a rush and a scrambling for notebooks when they saw him come up the steps – they had had a handout already, but they wanted some live quotes.

'Is it a fact that you don't intend arresting Johnson?'

'Isn't there a woman in this . . . ?'

'Was the plane smashed deliberately?'

Even now there would be photographers bumping out to Rawton Aerodrome, and in all probability getting lost in the dark.

But the reporters were not satisfied with details of *l'affaire* Johnson. Their professionally developed instincts warned them that this was only secondary. After exhausting all their questions they didn't rush off to the nearest phone, but instead returned to the waiting room, taking care to post a sentry. Then they picked up their cards again and automatically continued the game.

Having been through it once with them Gently had to repeat his performance for Walker, and the Super, like his man of parts, could see no alternative to the arrest of Johnson. Gently was masterful in his evasion, but he emphasized the salient point:

'That letter must have been sent by the culprit – and Johnson couldn't have sent the letter.'

'But suppose you leave the letter out of it.'

Gently shook his head decidedly. 'There are two factors concerning the letter which tie it directly to the crime. To start with, the paper was part of the same sheet on which Mrs Johnson painted her picture, and then the composer of the letter knew that Farrer had helped Johnson to escape.'

'Johnson may have lied about his movements.'

'I don't think he did, not in his condition.'

'You admit yourself that he's a clever bloke . . .'

'There's a limit to the cleverness that I admit to in anyone.'

Hansom, uncharacteristically, kept out of the argument. His belief in his judgement had taken a bad knock. He lit a cheroot in pretended boredom, and looked at the pictures in the Super's *Forensic Medicine* . . .

To avoid the reporters, Mallows was brought in by the back way, having been driven right round the block to evade passing the main entrance. He stalked fiercely into the office, a folded paper in his hand, but after some moments in the frigid room a lot of his starch seemed to go out of him. He looked tireder, older; there were dark semicircles beneath his eyes. His grey hair clung more limply over his distinguished forehead. But since nobody at first appeared to notice his arrival, he took a chair from the wall and sat down challengingly in front of the desk.

'A fine time of the day to drag a man out of his home!' His eyes rested on Gently reproachfully and without their customary twinkle. Then he glanced round the room at Walker, Hansom, Stephens, the stenographer, the latter busy sharpening pencils with a razor blade in a holder. The forces of society . . . ! Suddenly, Gently saw it all much clearer – as though, in a flash of sympathy, he was sharing Mallows's vision. They were arranged by accident in a crescent, resembling a primitive battle array; a formidable half moon of enemy figures who were no longer individual people. And at the focus, naked in his chair, the artist clutching that folded paper . . . Gently guessed that it was Mallows's *Times*, the innocent copy delivered to his house.

'We have some questions to put to you, Mr Mallows . . .'

Once more he was conscious of a painful symbolism. Always, the inquisition was started by the recitation of those words. He could hear Johnson's mocking rejoinder, speaking for everyone subject to question. 'Whacko . . . !'

Did one ever ask questions without implying an accusation?

'I know why you're after me – I saw what they found under my door mat. I was watching them, you can bet – you don't trust me, and I don't trust you!'

'Would you like to make a statement?'

'Damn it, yes, I'll do your work for you! No, sir, you can put your questions, but here's an answer for you to begin with.'

He threw his paper on the desk, making with it a stilted, jabbing motion; it was in fact the previous day's *Times*, his name scrawled roughly across one corner.

'You realize, naturally, that this proves nothing?'

'*Touché*, my friend. It proves I've got one.'

'Something suggested its use for a certain purpose . . . what would that be, except familiarity with the paper?'

'The knowledge that I took it in, perhaps.'

'Apart from your servants, who would have that knowledge?'

They were sparring like a pair of boxers trying to feel each other out: Gently instantly perceived his mistake, and let the next reply dangle in air. When the expected riposte failed to come Mallows stared at him, but maintained his silence. Walker, who was sitting at the end of the desk, also looked expectantly at Gently.

'Earlier today you admitted to certain knowledge concerning the recipient of a letter I showed you. You explained it by saying that he had telephoned you, but this he denies having done.'

'He might have very good reasons for that.' Mallows said it briskly, inviting a reply. Now, however, Gently was on his guard, and once more Mallows was left without support.

'Suppose I guessed it, knowing what I knew? One has a brain, and you can't help it working! From the letter one might deduce that it was Johnson who had eluded you, and after a quick check of suspects . . . surely Farrer is the obvious one? Naturally, Johnson would go to the bank. It'd be the last thing he would do. From there he'd want to get away quickly – and he was pals with Farrer. You see? It's deducible.'

'According to witness, you were more than friendly with Mrs Johnson.'

'Who told you that?'

'Is it true, or false?'

'It's true that people have different ideas of what is friendly – it's not the same thing in Mayfair and Montmartre.'

'You were more than friendly with Mrs Johnson.'

'I don't say you couldn't prove it.'

'She was your mistress for a time.'

'I'm going to swear at you, in a minute!'

Mallows was visibly put out by this form of procedure, which left him nothing to aim at and pinned him firmly to the defensive. His forte, as Gently had observed, lay in smart repartee, but deprived of openings for this he quickly surrendered the initiative.

'Derek Johnson suspected you of killing his wife.'

'If he did, then this is the first time I've heard about it.'

'He got in touch with you yesterday before he left the city.'

'My dear fellow, you're talking moonshine. I haven't spoken to him for days.'

'He got in touch with you from his office, and this is the gist of the conversation. In acknowledgement of his keeping his mouth shut, you were to pay him a certain sum of money. I'd better inform you that I've had an opportunity of talking to Johnson – at this moment he is lying in the West County Hospital, at Fosterham.'

Not only Mallows but the others also sat up at this outrageous statement, rolled out as it was with the most stolid conviction. Until then Hansom had continued his investigation of *Forensic Medicine*, but now he shut the book with a bang, his eyes opening wide.

'This is an astounding accusation!'

Mallows had flushed and was really angry: his big eyebrows lifted until they were nearly horizontal.

'It's not only astounding but untrue! I have had no communication with Johnson. If he says that I have, then bless my soul! The man is a psychopathic liar, and you can tell him I say so.'

'Then you didn't promise to pay him?'

'I tell you again, I haven't spoken to him!'

'He had no money from you?'

'Good lord! Am I going mad?'

'You didn't advise him to leave the country, undertaking to pay him ten thousand pounds?'

'A little more of this, and I'm going to insist on having a lawyer!'

'And yet you knew who received that letter?'

'It was only a guess . . . must I keep on repeating it?'

Gently paused for an instant, a gleam in his eye: now he

had produced a good working sweat! His next aim must be to keep it beading, to give Mallows no time to appreciate his tactics.

'Where did you have lunch on Monday last?'

'Monday . . . at home. I had lunch at home.'

'You had lunch with Mrs Johnson.'

'That's untrue. Until the evening . . .'

'According to witness you were seen coming out of Lyons with her.'

'Not on that Monday . . .'

'On that Monday! You went up The Walk with her and drove her off in your car. Johnson had been watching you, and he saw it too – so there doesn't seem much to be gained by denying it.'

'This is a fantastic perversion—!'

'Shall I tell you what followed? You told her that you couldn't pay her demands any longer. She'd been blackmailing you, hadn't she? Threatened to cite you as co-respondent! And for a time, till she got greedy, you thought it was worth your while to pay her.'

'You can't believe this!'

'Was she never in your studio?'

'Yes, several times, but—'

'You gave her that half-sheet of paper. You can't buy it in this country and only you had a supply of it – and precisely the same sheet was used for the painting and the letter! How are you going to explain that?'

'I don't have to – I won't explain it!'

'Yet you knew who received that letter?'

'For the last time – I guessed about it!'

Had the others got an inkling of what he was up to? Two

of them, at least, must be spotting the chaff amongst the wheat. Walker, on the other hand, was not so conversant with the details; he might be a little surprised, but he was probably swallowing most of it.

Under the glare of the strip light, his face looked frowningly intent.

'You were the last person to speak to her?'

'Have I ever denied it?'

'At lunchtime you called her bluff, and you were in purgatory until the evening. You hoped it would put a stop to her, that she would draw back from her threat – but she was determined, wasn't she? In a few words, she confirmed it. So you followed her, trying to soothe her, telling her that after all you intended to pay – that the money was in the car, that the car was in the park—'

'But it wasn't, it was in the Haymarket!'

'How many of your servants sleep in?'

'Two—'

'Above or below you?'

'Above!'

'So they wouldn't hear you go out!'

All the time he kept the tone subdued, never allowing his voice to rise: his face was entirely flat and gave no hint of the feelings behind it. He was like some impassive robot drilled to destructive accusation, turning it, twisting it to an implacable purpose.

'Last night you didn't sleep much.'

'I admit that. I had indigestion—'

'During the evening you concocted that letter, not to warn Farrer, but to make him tremble. At two a.m. you crept out of your house, carrying the letter and one of the knives. Where do you say you lunched on Monday?'

'At my house – the servants will tell you!'

'Why was your car parked in the Haymarket?'

'It couldn't have been!'

'So it was in the car park?'

'No!'

'Then where was your car? I thought you had decided it was in the Haymarket.'

'If you're talking about Monday evening—'

'Yes, Monday evening. Where was it then?'

'I can prove it was in the Haymarket!'

'And of course, you knew who received that letter?'

Mallows threw up his hands in despair. He needed time to recover his balance. He wasn't beaten – not yet; not by a long chalk he wasn't! – but Gently had got him persistently moving in the wrong direction. He badly needed a break to discover the pattern of this ruthless treatment . . .

'Didn't you tell me that Farrer was a friend of yours?'

'Yes . . . yes . . .' Mallows strove to hold him off.

'Goes to the same club – plays golf – exchanges visits?'

'Yes . . . that's right . . . I've met his family . . .'

'And this is the way you treat a friend?'

'What do you mean by that? I've always done my best—'

'If the positions were reversed, would he have treated you like that?'

'My dear fellow, regarding Farrer . . .' Mallows broke off with a hunch of his shoulders.

'You treated him shabbily! There's no denying that. The

whole trick was despicable, the product of an inferior mind. And you had the effrontery to admire it – to stand admiring those damaged pictures! In front of me, of all people, you showed the pleasure it gave you. There was a spectacle to arouse disgust and anger in the meanest of intellects, yet you, a distinguished artist, could only look about you and gloat . . .'

'Gently Iscariot . . . !' Mallows gave him a reproachful look, but Gently returned a marble stare and hurried on with his assault.

'Getting back to fundamentals – how long had she been your mistress?'

'I didn't admit that she had—'

'Oh? But we can produce several witnesses.'

'I categorically deny it!'

'That is your privilege, but the facts remain.'

'We were friendly—'

'So I understand – to the extent of her visiting you alone in your studio.'

'Twice – three times she came to my studio!'

'And after that she started the blackmail?'

'There was no blackmail—'

'We have evidence of that. And then again, you knew who received that letter . . .'

Two hours later it was still going on, in an atmosphere slowly thickening with tobacco smoke. Not once had Gently paused in his steady flood of accusation, and his low voice, varied only in tempo, seemed stamped on the character of the room. All of them were tiring except, apparently, Gently. The stenographer, who was only window dressing, had given up his pretence at scribbling.

Hansom was studying the ceiling, his umpteenth cheroot in his mouth; Stephens kept smothering yawns, and Walker was frowning harder than ever.

'And so, you knew who received that letter . . .'

That was the text of the fearsome gospel. Again and again it was punched at Mallows, till it began to take on an almost mystical quality. Sometimes the artist would try to counter it, wearily producing his argument of deduction; but this was no use, it was contemptuously shrugged aside, and always after an interval the words came again:

'But of course, you knew who received that letter . . .'

Hansom thought he would scream if he heard them any more. So the charlie *did* know who received the flaming letter! And what was so killingly funny about that?

An interruption came at last in the form of a buzz from the phone, and so absorbed had they been with Gently that everybody gave a start.

'Superintendent Gently here . . .'

Horrocks was ringing him from Chelmsford. He had discovered the lodgings where Johnson had claimed to have spent the night, and was able to confirm with near certainty that he had actually spent it there.

'It's only a small house with a spare bedroom to let. Johnson was in by half past ten and didn't leave again till after breakfast – round about eight-thirty; a taxi called for him.'

'Could he have left the house without their knowing?'

'Not without a load of luck he couldn't. The bedroom door sticks, there's a loose board in the landing, the stairs squeak like mad and the landlady has insomnia. Apart from that he could have jumped from a first-floor window, but if he did, he landed lightly enough on a bed of geraniums.'

'Did you get on to the cinema box office?'

'Yes. She remembers him by his tash. Also, we've got a record of two trunk calls to Lordham exchange.'

Thus Johnson was finally eliminated as the possible author of the letter and slashings – saving a miracle, he could not have been on the spot at the time. From the beginning Gently had not considered his claims very seriously, but while he remained, a credible door had stood open . . .

'Suppose we have some coffee now?'

The stenographer departed with alacrity. According to the office clock it was now past one a.m. Mallows, haggard, looking bemused, sat hunched and sprawling on his chair; his brilliant eyes were drooped and hooded, his finely boned hands hanging down beside him. How much further to go for the breakdown? Another hour? Another two, or three? Surely, by now, the artist could grasp its inevitability, could sense the undeflectable intent of his antagonist. He had nothing at all to gain: was it merely pride that made him hold on?

'Where are you spending your leave this summer . . . ?'

Over the coffee, Walker roused himself for a chat. For ten peaceful minutes there was conversation in the office, with Mallows, ignored, sitting listening or not listening. This was the usual thing, an acknowledged sleight of interrogation; you gave your subject a whiff of the normal life outside his nightmare. They were ordinary people, that was the gambit, they were only doing a job, it was foolish to give them trouble . . .

'Didn't I see that you'd won a prize in last year's angling competition?'

'I had a roach of just on three . . . it won it, against the national average . . .'

Stephens was showing Hansom his watch, an expensive self-winder of which he was proud: 'It was my passing-out present at Ryton . . . all the family clubbed together.'

For ten minutes – and then it was over, with everyone turning their eyes back to Mallows. How could he fail to have been impressed by such a performance? Now let him cooperate, and they could all go home to bed . . . !

'Don't you think it would help if you agreed to make a statement?'

Mallows shrugged his shoulders feebly, then shook his massive head.

'Very well, where did you have lunch on the Monday of last week?'

'At home. I lunched at home. Why don't you ring up and ask the servants . . . ?'

And so they were off again, on the second leg of the serial, with Mallows still game though obviously very tired. As a form of defence he began answering at random, apparently without caring what admissions he made. Perhaps he had noticed the inactivity of the stenographer. The latter was still engaged in drinking his coffee. After drawing a few responses which were tantamount to meaningless, Gently jolted the artist awake by introducing a fresh angle.

'Do you recall our conversation on Saturday?'

'On Saturday . . . ? Yes, I recall a conversation . . .'

'You made a number of suggestions to me relating to the crime.'

'Yes . . . that's right . . . I did make suggestions.'

'Knowing them to be false and completely misleading!'

'Hold on . . . my dear fellow! I was trying to help you.'

'You drew a plausible character of the murderer of Mrs Johnson, knowing, I repeat, that it was false and misleading.'

'No! You've got it wrong . . .' Mallows straightened his sagging shoulders. 'I gave you that in good faith, I wasn't trying to mislead you. At that time, without knowing . . .'

'Without knowing what?'

'I don't know . . . but I felt positive that Johnson hadn't done it.'

'You knew that he hadn't done it!'

'No, I didn't know that . . .'

'But you thought you would give me a will o' the wisp to chase after?'

'It was an intelligent appraisal—'

'From personal observation?'

'Yes, in a way . . . all appraisals stem from that.'

'So?'

'I don't know what you mean!'

'Who did you have in mind for that character?'

'It was imagined . . . a purely synthetic creation . . .'

'Designed to mislead me?'

'No – in good faith!'

'And since that time – Sunday morning, for instance?'

'That – that confirmed what I had suggested . . .'

'Confirmed it in what way?'

'Isn't that obvious? . . . A pronounced psychopath.'

'An artistic psychopath?'

'Yes – I suggested that all along.'

'And you admired the way he'd treated the pictures!'

'No! You can't contend that seriously . . .'

This line being started, Gently kept on repeating it – to the irritation of Hansom, who couldn't see it tending anywhere. It became almost as ubiquitous as the question about the letter, and appeared in a number of shapes and variations.

'You are well acquainted with Allstanley?'

'Yes . . . well acquainted . . .'

'You see a lot of him, do you? Outside the group meetings?'

'I wouldn't say a lot . . . he visits the studio.'

'How long have you been acquainted?'

'Oh . . . nine or ten years.'

'So you know him pretty well.'

'Yes, yes, pretty well . . .'

'Answer me yes or no! Is he the original of that character?'

'No – certainly not!'

'Where did you say you had lunch on Monday . . . ?'

Then, after a rest, the blackmail angle was resumed, urged with a venom and apparent authority that shook Mallows again from his apathy. At times, as the questions battered him, he seemed almost convinced of their justness: he had lost the will to protest, the truth could be whatever Gently cared to make it.

'Why should Johnson try to blackmail you?'

'I don't know . . . I can't think . . .'

'There could be only one reason!'

'Yes . . . I see that, of course.'

'You may not know it but he'd been following you – he had the necessary evidence.'

'Yes, I think it probable . . .'

'When did Mrs Johnson become your mistress?'

'She came to the studio . . . I don't know . . . !'

They had a second coffee break, the office clock now pointing to three. Hansom, who had got through his case of cheroots, had borrowed a packet of Players from Stephens. From the desk came a buzz for Gently – was he at liberty to talk to the press? The reporters were sweating on a break in time to catch the London editions.

'Tell them they'd better go home to bed!'

For the first time, he was lighting his pipe. The taste of it was bitter, it had an early-morning harshness. Soon, now, a wintry light would begin to soften the black window panes, and down below in the street a laden milk lorry would clatter by. Then the solitary cyclist and a pedestrian, his boots echoing, the mysterious early risers who began to wake the city; a greeting shouted out, the yelping bark of a dog, and far away, over the river, a cock's disembodied crow . . .

Mallows was offered a cup of coffee and he drank it in a sort of stupor; this time, there was very little effort at conversation. They were tired, and to be frank, discouraged; Gently's pressure was getting them nowhere – Mallows had been beaten into mental numbness, but seemed as far from a confession as ever. And what was even more discouraging, two of them knew that Gently was bluffing. Most of his reckless accusations had no evidential basis. He was applying sheer, brute force, and not, it seemed, with too much intelligence: it was a policy of obstinacy, savouring a little of despair.

And he was intending to go on with it – you could read

that in his face. Out of the perfect, masking blankness had grown a pertinacious expression. He was going on to the end, however far ahead it lay: he was locked in a struggle with Mallows which could only be finished by the collapse of one of them . . .

'Let's reconstruct the whole of last Monday. What time do you say you got up in the morning?'

Mallows had barely time to drink his coffee before Gently was pounding away at him again.

'I don't remember . . .'

'Was it eight? Was it nine?'

'No . . . half past seven . . . you'd better ask Withers.'

'I'm asking you! Now, when did you read her letter?'

'Her letter . . . ?'

'Yes – the one demanding money.'

'I never had such a letter—'

'Oh? Then how was it found in your bureau? It was dated as from the previous Sunday, and asks for an immediate advance of fifty pounds.'

'I repeat, I never had such a letter!'

'It is scarcely worth your while to deny it. Our handwriting expert will check it and there will be no question about his verdict. So having read it, of course, you rang her up, and suggested that she should meet you at lunch. But, in the meantime, you came to your decision: you weren't going to pay Mrs Johnson any more. Where did you park your car, by the way?'

'At the Haymarket—'

'At last, you admit it! I thought you were going to deny it again, and to go on swearing that you lunched at home. Then at what time did you meet her?'

'I didn't . . . I didn't meet her!'

'Then why were you seen together?'

'We weren't . . .'

'You were — I have witnesses to prove it. Your appearance is unusual, you know, and you'd be foolish to gamble on people not noticing you. And the whole thing fits so neatly. Later on, we have other witnesses.'

'I swear before God that I lunched at home!'

'Though admitting that you parked your car at the Haymarket?'

'That was later—!'

'Not by the accounts we have. You were parked there between one and two-thirty p.m. You occupied that time in having lunch with Mrs Johnson, and finally, according to witness, you drove off with her in your car . . .'

The clock marched on from three to four. Drably, the buildings across the way crept into relief. Mallows's condition grew worse than ever, and he seemed scarcely able to sit on the chair; he had come to the state when Gently's voice was growing meaningless, when the sharpest of questions evoked little response.

And Gently himself, he looked in little better shape, sitting hunched and small over Walker's desk. He was keeping his head propped up with his hands and his voice, usually clear, had become hoarse and thick.

'What reason could you have for trying to mislead me?'

'No . . . no . . . you don't understand . . .'

'You knew quite positively that Johnson was innocent?'

'No . . . I didn't . . . didn't know . . . not positively . . .'

'Was Seymour the person you meant?'

'No . . .'

238

'Aymas . . . ?'

'Didn't fit . . . couldn't fit . . .'

'Wimbush, perhaps . . . perhaps Baxter?'

'Not Baxter . . .'

'Wimbush?'

'Him neither . . .'

'What about Watts?'

'That too . . . ridiculous . . .'

'Yet you knew about the letter.'

'Yes, I knew . . . of course I knew . . .'

'How did you know?'

'I told you . . . guessed it.'

'How did you guess it?'

'Easy . . . easy . . .'

'Tell me how.'

'I've told you already.'

'Tell me again.'

'No . . . not again . . .'

'But I want to know how you guessed it.'

'Yes . . . I know . . . you want to know how . . .'

'What reason did you have for trying to mislead me?'

'Didn't mislead you . . . meant in good faith . . .'

Ponderously Gently relit his pipe, his movements seeming to come from some slow-motion film. For at least a minute he sat silently puffing, puffing, too exhausted, apparently, to form his usual smoke rings. Hansom watched him, bleary-eyed, Walker was unobtrusively napping; Stephens, to keep awake, was staring with eyes unnaturally wide. The stenographer, his pencils arranged fan-wise in front of him, lay back in his chair, his lids narrowed to two slits.

Gently rose to his feet and walked round to the front of the desk. He leant heavily against it, dropping a hand on Mallows's shoulder.

'It's time, perhaps, that I spoke more frankly . . .'

Mallows, with an effort, lifted up his head. Through the settling smoke of Gently's pipe Hansom could see the pair of them, eyeing each other.

'How did the letter prove that he'd done it?'

'You bastard, Gently . . . you out-and-out bastard . . . !'

'But it did prove it, didn't it? The paper was yours.'

'Yes . . . and you've known it all along . . . you devil!'

'How did he get it?'

Mallows gestured, feebly, helplessly. 'It was pinched from the studio . . . he studies papers, you know. I don't suppose he knew that I'd seen him take it, but I had . . . so as soon as you showed me the letter . . .'

'But you knew something before that?'

'Yes . . . everything . . . I told you. Then he wasn't at his car, though he left the cellar before me . . .'

'Why wouldn't you tell me?' Gently leant back on the desk: he neither knew nor cared whether the others could fathom this moment of truth.

'You may not understand it, but he's a decent fellow, at the bottom . . . I was probably his nearest friend . . . with me, he was like a child.'

'Yet you knew he couldn't go free.'

'It's not enough to know these things. You don't betray your friends because of the logic . . . only by blunders. That's how you betray them.'

'The blunders imposed by your conscience.'

'No, my dear fellow . . . no phrases . . .'

240

'You knew, and you knew you must tell.'

'I knew he was decent . . . who was I to condemn him?'

There was silence. Nobody stirred in the hazy, thick-aired office. The only motion was of the smoke which curled in tendrils from Gently's pipe. It seemed an age before Mallows, drawing his head up again, said:

'What happens now – are you going to pull him in?'

Gently slowly shook his head. 'Not now . . . he'll keep a while. I've had a man outside his house since yesterday morning.'

'He's a family man, you know.'

'Yes.' Gently pulled on his pipe. 'Perhaps, after the bank opens . . . myself, I'm not in a hurry.'

CHAPTER FOURTEEN

G ENTLY HAD RARELY felt so impersonal about the delinquent in a case and nor, as it turned out, was he ever to have less to do with one. Farrer was never brought to trial; he wasn't even arrested; in fact, while Mallows was still protecting him, there had ceased to be any Farrer. He had gone into his office and he had there quietly hanged himself. He had done it with some lighting flex suspended from a blind bracket.

He was smiling; that was a feature which added an especial touch of the macabre. His face wore exactly the expression with which he had been used to greet his customers. To perform the deed he had changed into his bank clothes, knotting with care his black bow tie; he had pinned some violets into his buttonhole and dressed his hair with a popular cream. Then, at around one a.m., he had stepped smiling from the window sill. His wife, who slept apart, hadn't missed him until breakfast.

'And what sort of a case did we have against him?'

Gently frowned when Superintendent Walker pinned him down with this question. Lack of sleep had made him bearish and his throat was painfully sore – he'd spent a quarter of an hour gargling it, and was still as hoarse as a crow.

'Not so good as the case we once had against Johnson . . . that's the reason why Mallows had to go through the hoop. But we could have built it up . . . perhaps got a confession. On the other hand, I doubt whether he'd have been fit to plead.'

To be truthful, the case against Farrer was slender, in spite of one or two circumstances that seemed most telling. It depended far too largely on the testimony of Mallows, and entirely so when it came to motive. But time, as usual, supplied a few clinchers. That was commonly the case when one had struck the right trail. Farrer, with all his cunning, had made some careless mistakes, and the most damning of these related to the paper knives. The second pair of knives he had actually bought in person. He had trusted to the likelihood that the supplier didn't know him. This was true, but the man had a good memory for faces, and he was quite able to pick out a photograph of Farrer. In addition:

'Just a moment! Doesn't this fellow manage a bank?' The picture had given a jog to a sluggish recollection. After searching through his files he came up with an order sheet: it was dated two years previously and bore Farrer's sweeping signature.

'There you are, I could have sworn that we'd done some business with him.'

The second item on the sheet was a stainless-steel paper knife.

Two more slices of luck followed one after the other. A

243

constable who knew Farrer had met him early on the Sunday morning. It was in Oldmarket Road and Farrer was proceeding towards the city, having just, without doubt, planted the knife and paper on Mallows. He had been striding along confidently and he had aroused no suspicion; according to the constable, he was whistling softly to himself.

More significant, probably, was the evidence of a cinema manager, who until he heard of the suicide had attributed no importance to what he had seen. Farrer had been noticed by this man on the night of the murder when, his last house being out, he had gone to the Haymarket for his car. Farrer was standing under a street light and intently examining his clothes. Then, extending his gloved hands, he had pored over these as well. The time was approximately five minutes to eleven, and the manager had driven away to leave Farrer still standing there.

But the corroborative evidence was to Gently by way of a bonus, and it was Mallows who supplied the really satisfying background. He had probed into Farrer's character during a long and intimate acquaintance, and had watched, with a clinical interest, the banker's relations with Mrs Johnson. It was a connection which boded tragedy but which had appealed to the academician's irony. His advice to Farrer had fallen on deaf ears and there was little he could do but observe developments.

'You couldn't foresee that something like this might happen?'

'Good lord, no! I was thinking in terms of a nervous breakdown. Farrer was always close to that – he was a chronic schizophrenic; one half of him was the bank man, and the other a frustrated Van Gogh. A jolly good breakdown was just what the fellow needed. It would have put him in the way of some psychiatric treatment. As I saw it, dear Shirley was going to break him to make him, and I didn't see any good reason for interfering.'

'You think he intended to walk out of the bank?'

Gently couldn't help feeling surprise at the way Mallows had taken that lambasting. Instead of making the artist shrink from him, it seemed to have roused his admiration; he appeared delighted, in retrospect, at the way Gently had got the better of him.

Now, on the Tuesday, when Gently had been scrawling out his report, Mallows had called to take him to lunch without even bothering to ring him first. The lunch had consisted of that missed fried chicken followed by an ice-cream meringue, which being eaten, they had taken their coffee and cognac to a swing sofa on the lawn.

'I'm certain he did. It was something he often spoke of. I made it a joke, but Farrer took it quite seriously. He was in Paris last year, you know, sort of spying out the land – he came back with a load of addresses, not to mention a caseful of literature.'

'Yes . . . we found it in his desk at the bank.'

'Did you? He showed it to me, at the time. Asked me if I'd ever had rooms in Montmartre . . . it was the Rue Lepic which seemed to take his fancy.'

'There were two addresses in the Rue Lepic.'

'Yes. It was just the sort of spot to attract Farrer. Then he asked me about cafés – where did one meet Picasso, etcetera – all the same, I thought it was foolery till I read the papers on Tuesday. But now, of course, I'm quite certain that he was proposing to leave, and that Shirley was intended to go along with him. When did you first begin to suspect him, by the way?'

'I don't know . . . when I found that his picture wasn't slashed.'

'That was a bad mistake, I agree, though completely typical of Farrer's make-up. And then?'

'And then the letter . . . how many people could have concocted it? In actual fact there were only two, and they were Farrer and Johnson. There might have been a leak – one or the other of them might have talked – but it was a very suspicious circumstance and it kept me thinking about Farrer.'

'After which I made my bloomer!'

'Yes, that practically put a seal on it. I was positive then that Farrer was the X of your description. It was incredible that you should have known what had happened at the bank, and there could only have been one other reason for supposing that Farrer had received the letter. You knew that he was the murderer. You knew that he had composed the letter.'

'Guessed, my dear fellow, in deference to protocol. I didn't see him do it and I didn't hear him confess. But, between you and me, I never had much doubt about him, and a glance at the letter disposed of any doubt I had. Yet how could I do it? How could I throw him to the wolves? I tell you again that, in spite of his failings, Farrer was a very decent fellow. He was human at his job – which isn't noted for the humanities – his employees all got on with him, so did his colleagues, and so did we. If his painting was a joke – and it was, behind his back – yet he was the first to reach

246

in his pocket when the Group was short of funds. Did any of the others run him down?'

Gently gave a shake of his head.

'No – they liked him, you see, whatever they thought of his daubing. The only reason why I was idiot enough to draw you his character was to stop you from nailing the job on Johnson.'

'Didn't you falsify his character?'

'Not I. How do you mean?'

'About the smile . . . I wouldn't have described Farrer's smile as being "shy".'

'Aha, my dear fellow!' Mallows winked at him delightedly. 'But it was the smile he used to me and not to his customers that I described. There was a difference, I admit, and you should have been clever enough to tumble to it. I caught you napping there – didn't I, Superintendent Gently?'

About his grilling he asserted that Gently would never repeat his success:

'You took me by surprise, you old devil, or we'd still be arguing the toss.'

And of the danger he'd stood in from Farrer, who had clearly suspected what Mallows knew:

'Now you're making it melodramatic – he'd never have dreamed of hurting me.'

Their conversation about the case drifted leisurely to other subjects, became a wandering, vagrant chat, in tone with the summer afternoon. They had found, each in the other, something that exactly suited their taste; and what better thing was there to be done than to talk at ease in the bird-haunted garden?

'You'll be going back, will you, to start on something fresh . . . ?'

'Yes . . . but I've got my holiday coming shortly.'

'Fishing, I thought you said?'

'I'm spending one week fishing, near Lynton.'

'And the other week?'

Gently shrugged. 'I'm supposed to be visiting my sister in Wiltshire.'

'My dear Gently! Spend it with me. I keep a houseboat on Burton Broad.'

It was arranged as easily as that. It needed no pressing or polite reluctance. Afterwards Mallows took him up to the studio, where a fresh canvas stood clamped to an easel.

'You see? I'm not entirely disinterested! I've begun a portrait and I want to finish it . . .'

On the canvas, blocked out in charcoal, was Gently caught with his far away smile.

The turn of events had been saddening to Stephens and his cup was filled when they were cheated of an arrest; he had wanted a resounding success so badly, the sort of success that one expected of Gently. He was also a little piqued about Johnson. His efforts there had been slenderly rewarded. Instead of the heroic capture of the murderer they appeared, indeed, as an indiscretion of youth.

'It wasn't even as though Farrer were a principal . . .'

Hansom, too, had made the same complaint:

'This boyo breezed into the case from nowhere – like somebody had pulled him out of a hat!'

Were they wiser as well as sadder? In Hansom's case Gently had his doubts; but Stephens, he decided, had learnt a lesson here and there. He himself had learnt something too. He felt his rank sitting easier upon him. He was still a rebel, always a rebel, but hadn't the world a great many mansions? And at heart, wasn't there a dash of the rebel in everyone?

Driving back, he came suddenly to a very solemn conclusion. It was time he sold the Riley, time he bought something a little newer . . .

Brundall, 1958.